THIS IS HOW YOU DO MAGIC, I REALIZE.
YOU READ THE STORIES IN EVERYTHING,
YOU SPEAK THE STORIES OF THE WORLD.

ALSO BY JIMMY CAJOLEAS

The Rambling

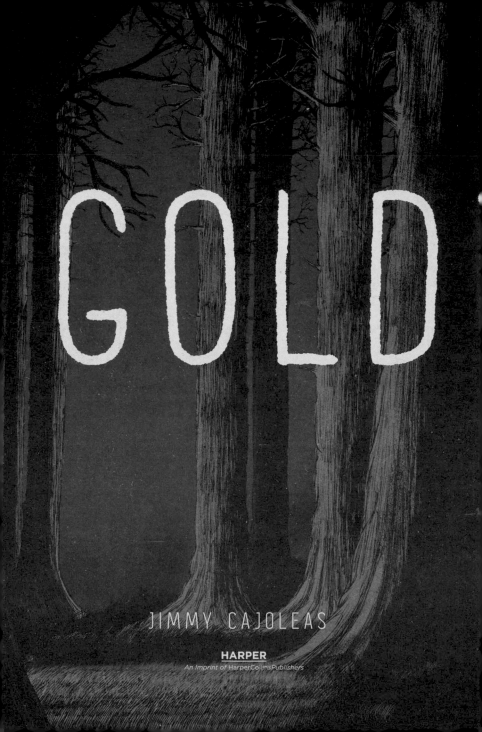

GOLD

JIMMY CAJOLEAS

HARPER
An Imprint of HarperCollinsPublishers

Goldeline

Copyright © 2017 by Jimmy Cajoleas

Illustrations copyright © 2017 by Matt Saunders

Library of Congress Control Number: 2017932861
ISBN 978-0-06-249876-2

Typography by Katie Fitch
19 20 21 22 23 BRR 10 9 8 7 6 5 4 3 2 1
❖
First paperback edition, 2019

FOR MOMMA

ONE

After the job, when it's all over, when Gruff lets me climb on his shoulders till I'm way high up with the leaves, the reds and greens and oranges, all the pretty colors, only then do I get to take off the cloak. Gruff always puts me on his shoulders after a job, after it's over and we're off celebrating, having a good time. Then I get to be his little girl again, his little Goldeline. But I got to wear the cloak till then.

I wait in the tree line, hiding, just a little off from the road. The woods are still and quiet, not a bird or a squirrel in sight, like the trees know something's going to happen, like the whole woods are waiting for it. Gruff and his men hide deeper in the trees, painted up and ready with their knives and hooks and swords, same as they've been all morning. It's boring, all the waiting around.

Plus it's stuffy in my cloak. Even fall here is too hot for something so thick and heavy. But Gruff says to wear it because it keeps me hidden.

"The cloak makes you look all derelict," Gruff says, "like a pitiful little orphan girl."

Which is what I am, I guess. But I don't like to think of it that way. Because I got people of my own. I got Gruff and his boys, the wild and free woods. I'm no orphan. I'm a bandit.

But here comes a carriage, so I got to go work now.

It's a black thing, shabby and hobbling, a long cart with a big canvas covering over it. That means they got something to hide, something worth something. Gruff's going to like that. The cart's drawn by two horses, and it's going pretty slow. The driver is a skinny man with gray hair and a mustache, smoking a pipe. He's looking up at the clouds, squinting at the air, like he's daydreaming.

Well, this should be easy.

I hop out of the woods into the road and let my hood fall down, and my hair spills out all white and lovely, "a splash of summer snow" Gruff calls it when he's being sweet. I've never seen snow except once, and it was just a piddly couple of inches that melted in a day. But I've seen my hair in a mirror before. Nobody I ever seen has hair like me, except my momma. I wave my arms at the driver and say, "Please, sir, stop. I'm lost. Help me." And the driver slows on to a stop because I'm only eleven and I don't look but ten, tops. If I was any bigger or older or rascally-looking, you can bet he would have run me right over.

The driver's a little spooked, you can tell. There's rumors about these woods, stories people tell of changeling babies and ghosty demons and dead white witches that go howl and moan with their torches in the night. Bandits too, the most fearsome in the land. But none of that can be me because I'm just a little girl, and it's daylight anyway.

"What can I do for you, little girl?" says the driver.

He's got no idea what's coming for him. The covering opens up and a man pokes his head out, red-faced and huffing. "What are you stopping for? Don't you know it's not safe to stop here?"

This man I know. I've seen him before. This man is a Townie, from Templeton, a tiny place in the Hinterlands. It's where I'm from too. I remember him from the last day. He was there for all of it. I remember his fat face screaming at Momma. He was right up front, right there next to the Preacher, one of the loudest Townies of all. You bet I remember him. When he sees me, his mouth falls open and his eyes get real big, like he knows exactly who I am too. Well, not *exactly* who I am, but close enough.

This isn't just going to be easy, it's going to be fun.

"It's the Ghost Girl," the man says, his face stricken,

aghast. "It's the Ghost Girl of the Woods."

I smile real big at him.

Gruff and the boys burst from the wilderness, some with their faces smeared with blackberry juice and some with bags on their heads that have eye slits and mouth holes outlined in red. They got knives and hooks and swords, and they have rags soaked in the tea I brewed for them, made from the forgetting herbs, the only bit of magic Momma ever taught me. They rush the cart all scream and holler, the horses bucking from fright, the whole forest done waiting, gone wild and exploded with demons.

This time I swear I'm going to watch, I'm not going to get scared and shut my eyes again. But at the last second I pull my cloak over my face and walk away, same as I always do. I cover my eyes and hide until Gruff and his boys have the Townie and driver tied up, until the forgetting herbs work their magic, until Gruff and his men have carried them into the woods. Sometimes the people come back from the woods, terrified, spewing wild stories about a Ghost Girl who let chaos loose around them, how they woke up in the woods days later with nothing but the clothes on their backs. Those are the lucky ones. Some people never come out of the woods at all.

It doesn't make me happy, but it does something else, like there's a horrible hurt deep in me that only this kind of thing can touch. The punishment of the Townies. Maybe it's justice—what they deserve—but really I just think it's revenge.

And revenge can be an awfully wonderful thing.

Gruff's boys tear through the carriage, upturn bags, dig for anything that could be traded, sold, or eaten. Sometimes a book for me, or even just something pretty.

"Hey, Gruff," says one of Gruff's boys. His name's Pugh and he's old and scraggly and only got one eye. Pugh doesn't like me much, which is fine by me, because I think he's the closest thing to wicked we got. Still, Gruff trusts him, so I guess I got to also. "You want to take a guess as to what all these barrels are full of?"

"I'd wager it's nothing less than the northern vineyards' finest," says Gruff. "A quality drink indeed. Illegal too, seeing as how the Preacher done banned the stuff."

He wipes some of the scary off his face, till he looks a bit more like my own Gruff. Tall and dashing, like a bandit king from a fairy story. He's fortyish maybe, with his hair going a little in the front and pulled into a long ponytail in the back. He's got a little bit of a gut too. But his mustache is long and elegant, and his forehead looks noble, his eyes laughing under the thick black eyebrows.

"Best to let me check it myself," says Gruff. "Wouldn't want one of my boys getting himself poisoned."

Gruff takes his knife and stabs it in the top of one of the barrels. He cups a hand in the rich dark purple of it and brings it up to his lips. Then he spits it out and makes a sick face.

"Chuck it," he says. "It's gone bad."

"Got to be kidding me," says Pugh.

"You'd think we'd get a break now and then. Just a little something to sip out in these woods, where it's so dull," says old sweet Leebo, wiping sweat off his forehead.

"Don't nothing ever go right for us," says Mince, whose dad was a butcher. He robbed half our knives from his pop's shop back in Templeton. "Luck of a bandit."

"Aw, I'm just messing with y'all," says Gruff. "It's the best we ever had in these parts. Guessing old Mr. Greencoats here was doing himself a smuggling business. Guessing he was trying to run this under the nose of the Preacher, make himself a little profit." Gruff cuffs another handful of the dark purple and slurps it like a dog. "Well, I figure we can say we were the instruments of justice for once."

"Yeah," says Pugh. "We carried out the law right and proper, didn't we?"

"Let's huff this junk back down to the camp," says Gruff. "A barrel to a pair of men. No whining. You'll be complaining plenty when all this is drunk up and you're wanting more. Gonna take us all day if we ain't quick about it. Come on now. Get to it."

"What should I grab, Gruff?" I say.

He jerks his head back to me, swift and fierce, like he forgot I was even there. He looks scary, lips purple, face smeared with berry juice, and for a second I'm scared, same as how Mr. Greencoats the Townie must have felt right when Gruff and his boys burst out of the woods. It makes me feel pretty low, if you want to know the truth about it. But then his face unscowls and his eyes soften and he wipes his mouth and he's my own sweet Gruff again, the one who took me out to the woods, the one who saved me. He bends down on a knee and looks me right in the eyes.

"Goldy, my angel," he says, "you ain't got to grab a thing. You just carry yourself right back to camp and see if you can get some of the other boys up and moving. Lazy bums might hop off their butts for once."

"Will do, Gruff," I say, and he laughs.

I like this part. I get to bring good news to Gruff's boys. "Blessed be the messengers," says the Book, "when the news is good. But woe be unto those who bring bad tidings to the King." I think I can ignore that second part for tonight. I know all about the Book from when I was little. It's rare folks even get to read a copy of the Book on their own. I hear most towns don't have but one copy, and that's the one that's locked up tight in the reliquary, where only the higherups can get to it. But me, I probably know more Book stuff than any other bandit in the whole woods. I take off the cloak and fold it over my arm, happy to skip my way back to the camp, singing the nothingsong Momma taught me, a messenger with nothing but good news to bring.

Tonight the camp is quiet. We're all pretty worn-out from the job today, even though we got some good stuff, even though we got plenty to eat tonight. Gruff's boys are talking, telling stories by the fire. About fifteen of them total, the good-for-nothings, that's what the Townies called them. All the lazy ones who never help with the jobs, who just loaf around all day. Gruff always says the only thing you can count on everyone showing up for is mealtime. We even got a couple of women too, like Murph, who's six feet tall and has one front tooth, and Lemon, who used to be Mince's wife. She's shorter than me but mean as a bobcat, and I'm a little bit scared of her.

Gruff just calls them all his boys.

You can hear a few men just out of the reach of the fire, and their laughter explodes from the dark like their own kind of light. Sometimes even Murph will sit me down and tell me a story. She looks tough but her stories are the best, about her days as a sailor slinking up and down the coastline, about storms at sea, about rogue waves higher than the treetops. I've never seen the ocean. I've never even seen a mountain.

Gruff comes strutting out of the tent in his evening robe,

a tattered velvet thing pilfered from some rich guy in a job a few months back. It doesn't fit him quite right, and his stained undershirt hangs tight over his belly. He's got a jewel-crusted flagon for a cup, and he's pouring good drink out into the nice goblets, passing them around to everyone. It's a reward for a job done right, even to the ones who didn't do a thing. You'd think we were the rich guys, all the stuff we got around here. I even have a decent library hidden in my tent. I keep every book that isn't too heavy or isn't all mucked up. Gruff smiles when he sees me.

Momma said I could trust Gruff, that he was a good man, as far as men go.

See, Gruff was good to Momma and me, sometimes gave us food when we didn't have any, potatoes and meat and vegetables, stuff he probably stole from somewhere. But Gruff was kind, and I can't really say that about much of anybody else I ever knew. That's why I took up with Gruff and his boys after the Townies killed Momma. The people in Templeton I mean. The Preacher and everyone wanted me dead too. The same wicked in her was in me, the Preacher said, on account of how we both had magic. Said he could see it in my eyes, gold-flecked, same as Momma's. That's why she named me Goldeline, because of my eyes.

After all the men are passed out, me and Gruff go off to a secret spot, a little clearing where there's a stream and a great big rock, where you can lie on your back and hear the trickle of water and feel the cool of the rock on you, where you can best see the sky. I'm tired and feeling a little bit lonesome, missing Momma, missing our hut in the woods where I was always safe, where I knew I would always belong. I look up at all the stars and point to all the pictures in them, the archer and the saint and the dog and the dippers, the birds and the dragons, the constellations I know already and the ones I just make up on the spot. It's a nice game, to draw pictures with the stars.

"Tell me a story," I say.

"What about, darlin'?" says Gruff.

"Tell me about Moon Haven."

"Lord, Goldy. Again?"

"Please," I say. "You don't even have to tell me a story about it. Just describe it to me. It's my favorite place in the world."

"Angel, you never even been there."

"That's why I need you to tell me about it again."

"A'ight," he says, sighing. "To start with, law don't take in Moon Haven. It doesn't know what to do with itself. That's why folks like you and me can get along just fine there, without any trouble. Gambling, circus animals, magic—the good kind, like what your momma had—anything you want, right there in Moon Haven. Right there in the heart of it, you know what they got? A courthouse? Heck naw. What they got is the most wonderful place of all."

"What is it?" I ask, same as always.

"What it is," says Gruff, "is the Half-Moon Inn. You never seen a place like it. I doubt there's any other place like it in the whole world. There's dancers, women who you wouldn't believe. Mermaids, I seen a mermaid there, they had her out on display. It was just a dummy of course, stuffed, because you could never yank a mermaid out of the water without her turning straight to dust. But you could see how pretty she would have been if she was real. You could see how a sailor would drown himself for her. And a lady with the whole story of the world tattooed on her body. You could read armies fighting, great battles and love and stars, all kinds of things written into her, from her neck down to her toes."

"They got stuff for girls there too?" I say.

"Sure thing. They got dresses, all colors, silk and everything else. They got seamstresses, they got madams serving tea and cake. They got dollhouses for days, a million different kinds of dolls, porcelain, all different kinds of hair, anything you want. A special place for kids to play with them while the grown folks go about their business. Whole barn out back full of bunny rabbits for girls to pet. What are you wanting with little-girl stuff anyhow? You ain't any little girl anymore. You're an outlaw, like me."

"Pretty big inn to have all that in it," I say.

"Shoot, it's the biggest inn in the Hinterlands. Tall as a

castle, but made out of wood. Got a flag with a skull and jewels for eyes on it, flies high over the whole woods. The doors are higher than a normal house, bear rugs all over the floors. Just like a king's palace in a storybook, I guarantee you. All you could dream of they got in the Half-Moon Inn. There's an old lady with no eyes who can read your future in a deck of cards. Speaks through her daughter, little blond girl, not too much older than yourself, by the name of Zemfira. You two would be friends, you and Zemfira would. She could talk to dead people too, anybody you want. Spirits, you know, dancing like little fires over your head."

"Could she talk to Momma for me?" I say.

"Course, Goldy, you bet. Could even talk to old dead Ajur Redbeard if you wanted, fiercest pirate that ever sailed. They got acrobats and knife-throwers and sword-swallowers and swashbucklers and Siamese twins, anything you could want is in the Half-Moon Inn. Could've spent my whole life in the Half-Moon Inn."

"Why'd you ever leave?" I say. "If I was there, I'd never leave. It would be my home forever."

"Well now." Gruff coughs. I like the way it rumbles in his chest, like he has a dragon hidden inside him, big and powerful and fire-breathing. "Guess I got crossed up a little. Cards, women, you know how it gets. Or maybe you don't. Heck, I hope you don't. Let me put it like this. Old Gruff took a fancy to a gal, 'bout nineteen, name of Helena

Gregg. She just happened to have herself a husband, not that I knew anything about it. Boy, he was a bruiser. Could break boulders with just his skull, that kind of guy. Like to whooped me into mush."

"How'd you beat him?" I say.

"Honey, here's something you got to learn, and learn it good. Sometimes you got to stand your ground and fight. Win or lose, take what's coming to you. Other times you got to turn tail and head for the woods. Like we done, after Templeton. No use fighting God and the law at the same time, a dangerous combination if there ever was one. No use getting pounded by some hillbilly husband over a little misunderstanding, know what I mean? Also, there was an issue with money."

"Money?"

"I'm not the best gambler there is. Always pay my debt. Eventually anyhow. Pay my debt when I can. I'm an honest man. Except for when that debt is so high dadgum royalty couldn't pay it. Again, sweetheart, that's when you pack your bags and slip out through the window. Shimmy down on your bedclothes. Get out in the darkness, leave not a track behind."

"I want to go," I say.

Gruff looks at me a little confused for a second, like he forgot we were talking about Moon Haven altogether.

"Course you do," he says. "And you'll get to, one day, mark

my words. When you're a real bandit, of course. Because only real bandits are allowed at the Half-Moon Inn."

See, Gruff doesn't think I'm a real bandit yet. I know Gruff's boys agree with him. Some of them—Pugh, Lemon, even old Buddo—laugh at me, still treat me like a kid, even though I'm the one who goes out in the road and waves down the carriages, even though I'm the only one who can mix up the forgetting herbs. So what if I get scared and have to close my eyes sometimes during the robberies? If it wasn't for me, for the Ghost Girl of the Woods, the Townies would know it's just flesh-and-blood people out here looting them, and then they wouldn't be scared anymore. In fact, they'd come after us. I'm the only reason we can survive in the woods. Sometimes it makes me so mad I could spit.

But when I make it to the Half-Moon Inn, that's when Gruff will know I'm a real bandit, not just some lonesome little kid. That's where real bandits belong. That's where I'll be home. Until then I'll live on the road with Gruff and the boys. I'll be part of a wilder story, the kind of thing you tell kids at night to scare them. I'll be what they fear most, the Ghost Girl of the Woods, the one who can curse the Townies, the one who when you see her it means death. I'll be the one they are all scared of, the one they see in their dreams to let them know it's gonna be a bad one. I'll get my own revenge on the Townies.

A bandit. That's what I'll be, through and through. And a

bandit's what I'll always be, forever.

"Let's get on back now," says Gruff. "We got to up and move camp early tomorrow morning."

"Again?" I say.

I liked this spot. I think it's my favorite campsite we've had in months.

"'Fraid so, Goldy," says Gruff. "It wouldn't do to have folks find out where we're hiding, now would it?"

"But the Townies don't think we exist, remember? I'm the Ghost Girl of the Woods!"

I throw my arms up and wiggle my fingers all spooky like, hoping Gruff gets a kick out of that. But Gruff doesn't much look like laughing.

"Townies ain't all I'm worried about," he says.

I know exactly who he means, and it shivers me down to my bones.

"You won't let the Preacher get me, will you, Gruff?"

"Not on your life, Goldy," he says. "Gruff'll good and protect you just fine. Now go on and get you some rest. We got us a big day tomorrow. Got lots to carry, thanks to your work today, and miles and miles to carry it."

I walk with Gruff back to the camp, singing soft to myself, the moon high and bright above us. The moon is always a mystery, always a secret the sky tells. That's what Momma used to say. Momma had a lot to say about the moon, about its pull on you, about what the moon will let you do, how if you talk to her she'll make your hair shine with the dew. It's true too. Momma never once lied to me, not that I ever heard.

Momma trusted Gruff, so I do too. If Gruff says he can keep me safe from the Preacher, then I believe him.

TWO

We wait only two weeks till we're out again. I don't like this so much. For one, it's too soon. We always wait longer between jobs, at least three weeks, so maybe folks put their guards down a little. But the boys ate up the food too fast, and there wasn't much gold to be had from Mr. Greencoats. We haven't had a good meal in a whole week. Gruff was real grumbly when I mentioned it to him.

"You think I don't know that, Goldy?" he said. "Lord, you're complaining too. You and everybody else. Who do they want in charge? Who can do a better job than old Gruff?"

That made me feel real bad, like I wasn't grateful. That's why I didn't complain about the new spot either. See, we move to a different place on the trail every couple of jobs, just in case folks get wise to us. I don't like this new spot Gruff picked at all. It's at a twisty, windy part of the trail, right past a curve where you can't see what's coming. I guess that's the point, that the carriage can't see me until the last minute, but it sure makes me nervous. If the carriage driver doesn't notice me in time I could get squished. I hate that Gruff picked this spot but I don't say a thing to him about it. I don't want him knowing that I'm scared.

Because I am scared. The sky is all gray and there aren't any good birds out, just crows and dark things. There's a bad taste in the air, like something died too close, like maybe far away someone's cooking something awful. It's hard to explain I guess. Sometimes I just get these feelings that start way down in my toes and crawl up me like ants. It's a bad tickle, a warning. But bandits don't get scared, not real ones. I sing Momma's nothingsong and try to spook the bad feelings away.

A cardinal lands on a twig above my head. It sings its little harp song. I think it's the brightest thing in the whole woods today. Momma said not to trust cardinals because they're vain and they don't ever tell you the truth but I think they're pretty. This cardinal hops up and flies away, leaving the tree branch all alone, and I miss it already.

Right then a carriage comes down the road. It's a fancy thing, with two big brown horses trotting out front. Must be a rich person. I bet they got all kinds of food in that carriage, gold and pearls and wine. I bet they got velvet lining. I bet they got everything a person could ever want stuffed in there.

I step out of the woods into the road and let my hood fall down like always. I wave my arms and say "Help me!" extra loud so I don't get run over. The driver's a short, paunchy man with his hat pulled low. He slows down a little, eyeing me weirdly, but it doesn't look like he's going to stop for me. But then a lady sticks her head out of the carriage door. She has red hair piled up in braids on top and her dress is all frilly, like what you'd wear to a ball. She's kind of pudgy and she smiles real big.

"Slow down, James, slow down," she says. "There's a darling little girl out here, and she seems lost."

"No good stopping in these woods," says the driver.

"I didn't ask you your opinion," says the lady. "I asked you to stop."

"I heard tell of a ghost girl that haunts these woods. Heard tell of bad things that happen for them that stops."

"Don't be ridiculous," says the lady. "There aren't any ghosts. Now stop the carriage before I have to jump out myself."

The driver slows the horses until they stop right next to me. The door opens and the lady steps herself out and bends down to me. She's not a Townie, not one I've ever seen before. For one, she's dressed too nice. Also, she doesn't have that nervous look all the Townies have ever since the Preacher showed up, like somebody's always watching them, like they're scared of getting caught. This lady's probably never even been to Templeton. She just made a bad decision about what trail to take today.

"What's wrong, dear?" the woman says.

She seems like a nice lady and I feel real bad about it.

When Gruff and the boys come screaming from the woods, I don't even try to watch. I shut tight my eyes and stop up my ears with my fingers and count to one hundred. It usually doesn't take any longer than that.

When I think all the bad is done and over with, I open my eyes. Pugh and Dunce are tying up the woman and her driver, both passed out from the forgetting herbs, from my own magic. All you do is crush the leaves up, then pray over them while you make tea. People don't remember anything, not a bit. Gruff's boys will carry them out deep into the woods and leave them there. It hurts me to see the nice lady slumped over like that, her hands bound, all weak and helpless.

A big trunk is tied to the back of the carriage. Gruff dumps it out and he and Murph start digging through it.

"Coins, some bread, some drink"—Murph pops the cork, takes a swig—"even got grapes in here."

"Goldeline," Gruff barks, "can you hop in that carriage and see what you find?"

I don't answer him.

"What's the matter? Shoot, I'm sorry," he says. He wipes all the mean off his face and smiles at me real big and he's Gruff again. "See, it's just me." He bends down and ruffles my hair, and I feel a little better. "Goldy, will you check the inside? Me and Murph here are busy at the moment."

I love Gruff, I really do. He's my own Gruff and he takes care of me better than anyone ever has, except for Momma. I'd be dead if it wasn't for Gruff. The Townies would have got me. Their ugly red faces, calling Momma wicked, even though some of them used to come by at night, for medicine or for other things. When the Townies came Momma always made me go outside, even if it was late-late. Momma didn't want me to see such people in pain. Besides, some matters ought to be private. So she gave me a lantern and I got to walk in the woods and look for owls and raccoons and all the night creatures that wake up with the dark. When I got scared I would sing the nothingsong Momma taught me and then I wouldn't be scared anymore. She'd put a candle for me in the window I could see for half a mile, a glowing cat's eye in the dark to call me home.

"Goldy," says Gruff. "The carriage."

"Right. Sorry, Gruff."

This isn't my normal job. Most of the time I just look innocent and get the carriage to stop. But only three of Gruff's boys showed up today, and I have to do extra to help. The rest are all at the camp, loafing, waiting on Gruff to bring back food or money. But even if all the boys leave and it's just me and Gruff I'll stick by him and one day we'll go to Moon Haven and be happy forever together.

The carriage is fancy. Velvet curtains, pillows on the seats. Rich stuff. Not much we can use though, just knickknacks, some sewing things, a stiff-bound book too heavy for my pack. I don't know why, but it seems like it belongs to happy people, like these are the things you get to have when you're a person with a family.

But then something wonderful happens.

I pick up a blanket bundled on the floor and there's a boy with bright-red hair hiding underneath. Like a changeling boy from a fairy story. He's got both hands covering his mouth, trying to keep from crying out. He's my age, I think. A little younger. He looks at me with the scaredest eyes, and it makes me remember the awful day when Momma died. I look into his eyes and I know just how he feels because that's how I felt that day too.

I stop for a good long minute. Then I do something maybe stupid. I know I shouldn't, I know Gruff would beat me raw, I know I'm putting us all in danger, that what I'm about to do is permanent, can never be undone, and maybe it'll ruin everything. But I can't help it. It's like there's a little voice in me that sings, *Look in his eyes, Goldeline. He's just the same as you.*

I stick my head out of the carriage and check to see if Gruff's looking. He's not, so I drop the blanket back over the boy.

"Don't move for a really long time, okay?" I whisper.

I walk over to Gruff and tug on his shirtsleeves.

"You find anything?" he says.

"Nope," I say. I say it just like I'd say it if it were the truth. See, I'm a real good liar.

"Well I did," he says. Gruff pulls a white dress from the trunk. It's so pretty you could call it a gown. It shimmers and sparkles in the sunlight. I never seen anything so beautiful in my life.

"For me?" I say.

"For you," he says.

I can hardly believe it. It's the finest thing anyone has ever given me.

"You hang on to that dress now. Don't let it drag in the dirt." Gruff turns to Dunce and Buddo. "Let's get out of here. I'm starved."

"Hey, Gruff?" I say.

"Yeah, Goldy?"

"If it's okay with you I'm just going to walk around by myself for a bit."

"Sure, Goldy." He bends down on a knee and looks me fierce in the eyes. "Just don't cross the road, off into those other woods. Nothing there for you. I don't want to be crawling around the woods all dadgum night looking for you. And if you hear anybody coming down this way you make a run for it. Keep to the trees where they can't follow you. You hear me?"

"I'll be careful."

"Let's go, boys," says Gruff.

"Hey, Gruff?"

"Yeah, Goldy?"

"What's on the other side of the road? Ghosts?"

"Yep," he says. "And worse."

"What's worse than ghosts?"

"You remember the stories, Goldy. I told you a million times."

"Tell me one more."

He sighs. "It ain't just ghosts out there, though there are plenty of those. Dead bandits who never stopped robbing after they died, drowned women come up with lungs full of black water. But there's worse stuff than that, stranger stuff, wilder stuff."

"Like what, Gruff?"

Gruff looks at me serious, his eyes gone fierce.

"Bad people, Goldy. Folks who ain't got any code. Folks who will skin you alive just as soon as wink at you."

"That's why you won't let me cross to the other side of the road, to those other woods?"

"That's why. Now hush up. We got to get to camp and get

some grub. All this action's got me hungry."

They walk back into the tree-line dark.

When they're gone, I hang the dress on a tree branch so it won't get dirty and climb a bent limb up high and wait. Below me the dress flows and dangles in the wind like a lady's in it. A dancing ghost lady in her white dress out for the night, all the ghost music us breathers can't hear.

I shut my eyes until I see blue butterflies under my eyelids and sing the nothingsong so quiet the wind won't bother to blow it anywhere. I do something I don't do a lot. I pray to Momma to help. That's the kind of thing that the Preacher will burn you up for, blasphemy, even worse than the robberies Gruff has done.

I hear little footfalls in the road like a squirrel scamper and I open my eyes and it's the boy. He stops dead still and glances over his shoulder, like he's worried Gruff is still out in the woods, waiting for him. He runs again, but pauses at the dress. I look down on him from up in my tree and it makes me sad. See, it's probably his momma's dress, not mine, and it never will be mine. Not really. That's the problem with stealing, with being a bandit. Everything you got is really someone else's.

The wind twirls the dress on the branch. He reaches out to touch the sleeves but I want the dress for me so I grab a twig off the tree and snap it in two. It cracks like a rifle shot in the silent woods.

The boy screams and runs down the road toward town. I watch him till he's almost gone. I know what it's like, being alone in the world, scary things everywhere. I know just what it's like. If I let him go, he'll find his way to town fine, so long as a bear or something doesn't get him. There's only this road, and it only goes one way. It's better if I let him go on to town. But I can't. I don't know why. It's the same little voice that made me keep him safe in the first place, a little thing chirping away in my heart. I can't let him go.

"Hey, little boy." He runs faster, so I yell in my best Gruff voice, "Stop right there if you know what's good for you."

The boy freezes. He's shaking. I know it's bad, but seeing him do what I say is kind of fun. I get why Gruff likes being the boss, having power over folks. It's something I've never had before. This boy will do anything I tell him to.

"Turn around real slow," I say.

He does as I say, the whole time looking around like he can't find me.

"Up here, stupid," I say.

When he sees me his eyes get big. Snot's all dribbled down his chin and his cheeks are dirty and red from crying. He's actually younger than I thought, maybe about nine, two years younger than me. It's hard to tell though. I've seen roughneck toddlers from the country who look tougher than a rich thirteen-year-old.

"They took them out to the woods," he says. "I'm the only one left."

"I know," I say. "I saved you."

"Are you an angel?"

"An angel?"

"Aunt Barbara says there are angels all around. She says they're mostly invisible but sometimes they can be anybody. Even gross old Mr. Sellers down the road could be an angel in real life."

I've been a ghost for a long time, but I've never been an angel before. Maybe it'd be better to be an angel. Something pretty that people love instead of just being scared of. A ghost means death, but an angel protects people. A guardian angel. I could be that, just this once. It seems like fun.

"Yes, little boy, I'm your angel. What's your name?"

"How come you're my angel and you don't know my name?"

"I know your heaven name. Not your earth name."

"What's my heaven name?"

"If I told you, I'd get cast out of heaven forever. They'd rip my wings right off, like the Cursed Ones in the Book. Not to mention a demon would come drag you under the dirt all the way to hell and stab you with pitchforks for the rest of always. You wouldn't want that, would you?"

"A demon?" he says, eyes big and scared.

"What's your name?"

"Tommy," he says. "Aunt Barbara says my momma's an angel. That after she died she went up to heaven, same as my daddy. That they're angels together in heaven, waiting on me. Do you know my momma?"

I was right, I knew it, I could see it in his eyes. He's an orphan too. He's just like me.

"No, I don't know your momma. But there's lots of us angels out there. I probably just haven't bumped into her yet."

"Well, she's still new up there. She's only been an angel for a few months. That's why I'm going to live with Aunt Barbara. That's why I had all of Momma's stuff with me, for Aunt Barbara to remember her by."

"Was Aunt Barbara the lady in the carriage?"

"Nope. That's just her friend, Miss Lyons. Aunt Barbara lives in Carrolton." He looks at me funny. "For an angel, you sure don't know much."

"I knew enough to save you from those bandits," I say, crossing my arms. "And they might be heading back this way any minute. Wouldn't doubt it, not for a second."

Tommy whips his head around, gazing deep into the woods, scared all of a sudden.

Looking down the road, all I see is a gold ribbon of empty dirt. I don't understand being scared in these woods. The dark and scratching noises are nothing but deer and possums and raccoons, owls and mice, even sometimes foxes, who are lucky. Nothing really to be scared of here except us bandits. Better than the town full of wicked, jabbering crones and rat-toothed men. All the rich kids that hate you.

I make a big show of swooshing down out of the tree, branch by branch, slinging my hair like a ghost shadow behind me. I hold my hand out to him. "You better come with me. Otherwise the bad guys might come back and kill you dead with their hooks and their hammers. Come with me and let's get you something to eat."

He takes my hand and we walk through the woods and back toward Gruff's camp.

I hope I know what I'm doing.

The path is old, from way before me and Gruff ever wandered these woods, the kind that is cut and forgotten, the good kind. You can barely stand up, the trees are so thick and low. The branches form a roof almost as thick as thatch, and when it rains only tiny droplets get through. You could dodge them and never get hit. The water pools in the curve of the leaves and you can sip from them if you want.

I stop us at a tiny clearing out from the main trail, maybe half a mile from camp. The boy is slow and he keeps crying. He says his shoes are hurting his feet. I tell him to go barefoot, like me, that it'll make his feet tough, but he doesn't like that.

"Just you wait here, okay? I'll be back with food in just a minute. But don't go anywhere."

He stares at me with his face all dirty.

"What's the matter?"

"It's dark. And there are noises." The tears start again. "What if the bad guys come back for me?"

"Jeez, you're a scaredy-cat. I never met a kid so scared in my whole life." He just cries harder. "Okay, well. Let me teach you a song. To keep off the bad things." And I sing him the nothingsong my momma taught me. I make him sing it with me, his voice almost as high as mine, until he knows it. He learns it real fast, and his fingers move at his side like he's playing a piano.

"Just keep singing until I come back, okay?"

He nods but doesn't stop singing.

"Good boy."

When Tommy can't see me anymore I cut back out toward the road. I walk awhile back to the robbery spot. The carriage is gone, the horses trotted back toward town I guess. The dress still dangles in the tree. I snatch it off the branch and it tears a snitch at the shoulder. Too bad. Maybe I can fix it back at the camp.

THREE

It's darktime now and the moon is out, barely, just a moon smudge. Bats fling themselves through the trees and are gone like dark falling stars. At night the woods come alive, all the hidden things scurrying in the black. What is either fireflies or ghost eyes. They glimmer and blink away and I'll never know.

I left Tommy in a safe place, but I need to hurry. I figure I should be able to sneak some food out and be gone in no time. I walk faster, feeling my way by memory and moonlight. I know we'll have to move camp again soon, but I hope we get to stay here for a little bit longer. Right now is the best camp we've ever had. It almost feels like a home. Soon I can hear the music, and when I break into the clearing I can already smell the beans cooking, and I see all Gruff's boys.

Lemon hobbles past, grunting at me, lugging wood toward the fire. I nod at her like nothing's different.

Gruff's got his robe on, but it doesn't seem soiled tonight. It looks regal, like Gruff's an old fairy king, even down to the purple of his teeth. The men are up and dancing, the music good and wild. Old Andrew, with his three-foot beard and accordion, one-legged Leebo, with his crutch and viola, and old Mister Marty, with his goiter and his story songs.

"How are you this fine evening, Goldeline, my dear?" says Leebo, bowing for a flourish.

"I'm just fine, Leebo. Glad you got your music going."

I figure now's a pretty good time to go try on my new dress. I'll put it on and dance around a little and say hi to everybody, and then I'll sneak the food off for Tommy. I hope he can wait. I hope he won't get too scared. I hope nothing bad happens to him when I'm not there to protect him.

This time the camp is hidden in a clearing in the thick heart of the woods. No one could ever find it unless they knew where to go first or were just plain unlucky. Lord knows how Gruff got to it. There's all kinds of thornbushes round about the edges, and in the mornings after a big night they have blood on the prickles where the men went off to pee and fell. There's about nine or ten tents in all, just patchwork stuff we slung together, and a fire pit in the middle. When we have to move again, the whole camp will be up and ready to go in an hour. Gruff's tent is the biggest because he's the leader. It has two whole rooms in it with a long canvas sheet to separate them. Gruff calls one his "war tent" because that's where they're supposed to plan the jobs and discuss strategies, but mostly they just play cards in there. The other is the one where he sleeps. He's even got a mattress, not just a pallet full of feathers and leaves like the rest of us. My tent is the smallest. It's so small only I can fit in it, and even I can't stand all the way up inside.

In my tent I have a mirror with a gold handle that Gruff got for me, and my pile of books. I have the shawl I wore at Momma's trial but I don't want to talk about that. I sleep with the shawl under my pillow and smell it sometimes hoping it'll smell like Momma, but it only ever smells like ashes.

I light a candle and try out my gown. It doesn't look too good in my mirror. I'm not big enough, and the dress sags down my chest. Worse, I'm too short and there's no way to keep it from dragging in the dirt. I feel like a dress-up doll. But then, maybe, in the right moonlight, with the campfire glow on me, maybe it'll do. When I walk out of the tent, the hem follows me like a ghost shadow.

Gruff claps his hands. "Boys, don't she look gorgeous? Ain't our Goldy the northernmost star?"

"She's a doll," says Buddo. "Like one of them rich-girl dolls that blink their eyes."

"I'm no doll," I say.

Gruff about falls out laughing. "Hear that, Buddo? She's no doll."

"Geez, sorry. Shoot, Goldy, you know I didn't mean nothing by it," says Buddo.

"It's okay," I say. "Just don't do it again."

"Ought to stick her in an orphanage," says Pugh.

"Knock it off, Pugh," says Gruff. "That's my Goldy you're talking about, good as my own. Besides, she helps out on the jobs. She earns her keep, don't she, boys?"

"A straw dummy could do her job," Pugh mutters.

"I'll do you a right good job," I say.

All the men laugh.

"I wouldn't cross this one, Pugh!" says Gruff. "She'll stick you, she will. She'll get you right and good in the end!"

"She's a brave one for her size, she is," says Murph, tipping her glass to me, and I blush a little.

"We'll see," says Pugh, and then he wanders off away from the fire.

Gruff gets down on a knee in front of me. With his scraggle beard, his earrings dangling, he looks like a gentleman pirate from a storybook.

"You look pretty as your momma in that dress," he says. "God rest her soul."

It makes me go cold and warm at the same time. It makes me so happy it hurts and so sad I could die. I feel it all over me like a warm coat, like sadness and pain might swallow me whole. It's the nicest thing anyone's ever said to me.

Gruff grabs my hand and the music starts and we get to dancing. My dress floats and whirls around me, and I spin so the hem never touches the ground. This is a bandit night at its best: the glow and the warmth of the camp in the dark woods, the light of the fire and us singing and dancing and hollering around it, the people songs and the nighttime songs and our laughter all mixing together into something new and hopeful, a kind of promise, or maybe a wish. An owl hushes us from the trees up where I can't see any owl but I know it's there watching me. I wonder what the owl thinks of us. I wonder what Momma would think of me, dancing and all dressed up, her own daughter a bandit?

I hope she wouldn't be too mad at me. I hope she'd see me and smile.

Soon I'm laughing as hard as the rest of them. We dance and we twirl and I've never felt like this, never felt so pretty in my whole life. All the boys are out clapping and dancing and singing, and me and Gruff are the stars. Everyone is watching us spin around the campfire, us ghosts and legends, the ones all the Townies are so scared of. It feels wonderful to be a ghost, to be as pretty as Momma, as white-haired, lovely and dancing before a fire. It's a good time, when there aren't many. I bet this is what Moon Haven is like all the time, how it is in my dreams. It's all I want for forever. But I can't stay. I got to get back to Tommy. What if he's scared? He's just a kid. He doesn't know anything. And I left him out there in the woods all alone.

I tell Gruff I got to pee and sneak off to the tree line. Dunce is dozing by his tent with a whole bowlful of beans, and I take it without him even noticing. Keeping a close eye out for one-eyed Pugh, who hates me, who could ruin everything, I sneak my way out of the camp and run as fast as I can all the way back to the tree where I left Tommy.

When I get there, Tommy's curled up like a pup, whimpering.

"I couldn't scrounge up much," I say, "but I got you some real nice beans."

"I thought you left me," he says. "I thought you weren't coming back tonight. I thought I was going to get all eat up by wolves."

"There aren't any wolves here, stupid," I say. "Maybe some coyotes, but they won't do anything except ruffle you up a bit. Nope, worst you got to worry about eating you up is mosquitoes."

"You don't talk much like an angel," he says.

"Well how the heck are angels supposed to talk?" I ask.

"I don't know. Not like that."

"You ever met an angel before?"

"Nope."

"Then shut up about it. I'm an angel and I say whatever

I want," I say. "Anyway, are you going to eat these beans or what?"

I hand him the bowl and he sniffs it.

"Smells like something died in there."

"That's a heck of a thing to say, Tommy. You know this grub here is a gift from God, right? Like the Book says, 'If you refuse the gifts of the Lord, you refuse the Lord as well.' You refusing the Lord, Tommy?"

"No, ma'am," he says, and he gets to eating.

"That's what I thought," I say, but I'm smiling. *Ma'am!*

"Can I ask you a question?" he says.

"Shoot."

"Why are you wearing my momma's dress? It was her favorite thing, and Aunt Barbara wanted to keep it."

I forgot about the dress. I look down and it's all dirty and torn from the path. It hardly even looks like the same pretty thing I had earlier.

"God told me to wear it."

"Why'd he do that?"

"I don't know. He's God. He can say whatever He wants and you just got to do it anyway."

"I guess."

Tommy starts to crying again. I can't blame him. I cried for a whole year after my momma died. I still do sometimes, when I know Gruff isn't watching me and there's no one around.

"Hold up a minute," I say. "I'll be right back."

"Don't leave me," he says.

"Be brave for a little bit, okay?"

See, right by this spot there's a bunch of blackberry bushes. Sometimes I come up and sit in the tree and read my book and eat fistfuls of blackberries all day. I pick some and run them back to Tommy. He takes one and eats it and smiles a little bit.

"Good, huh?"

"I was scared you were going to leave me again."

"I'm not going to leave you, all right? I'm your angel. I'm here to protect you. For now, anyways."

"I thought angels stuck with the same person forever," he said.

"Think we've established you know squat about angels," I say.

A lightning bug dangles its glow over my face and hushes. I cup it softly in my hands.

"Hey, Tommy, watch this."

I pray a silent prayer to it: *please don't hate me for this, lightning bug, I just got to borrow your light.* I squish it in my palms and bury my face in the goo. When I look up Tommy screams.

"You're glowing!"

"I know! Watch!" I catch another one and smear its light over Tommy's cheeks. He rubs them and a snatch of glow sticks to his finger. Then he darts off into the dark.

"Tommy? Wait, this isn't funny. Where'd you go?"

I chase after him but I can't see him. He jumps out from behind a tree. He doesn't scare me but I fake a yell.

"Ha! I gotcha."

I chase him and he chases me and pretty soon we're cackling and screaming, our faces glowing like stars. Tommy trips over a tree limb and I tackle him and we both fall down laughing, which pretty quick turns into crying, and me and Tommy cry each other out on the roots and tangles and dark wild earth of the woods.

I wake up with the daylight. Tommy's munching the last of the blackberries, teeth as purple as brand-new grapes. It's shady and cool under the tree. All the day bugs are waking up, whirring into the light. A fawn and two baby deer walk by, stepping soft as ghosts. Tommy whistles and they bolt off, gone quicker than a happy thought.

"You spoiled it," I say.

"Deers got ticks on them," he says.

"How would you know?"

"Sure do taste good though. My daddy used to shoot a deer any chance he got."

"What was your daddy like?"

"He was the tallest, bravest guy you ever met. I one time saw him arm-wrestle a riverboat captain and he beat him in no time flat."

"When did he die?"

"Three years ago, when I was seven."

Tommy's ten? That's only one year younger than me. He acts like a six-year-old. His voice is all high and he cries all the time. If he were Gruff's boy, Gruff would whoop his butt right into being a man.

"That's right," I said. "Three years ago. Hard for me to keep it straight."

"Why's that?"

"Heaven time don't work the same as earth time, Tommy. A day with God is like a thousand years, don't you know that?"

"Never heard that one before. A whole thousand years?"

"Doesn't feel that way," I say. "Sometimes it passes quick as a summer morning. Other times it's like a cold winter night that won't even end. Heaven time is a tricky thing."

It's fun being an angel. Good thing I know so much about the Book. I remember how Momma used to read me fairy stories, and Gruff would tell me all about the ghosts of the woods. But I feel like I grew up knowing the Book like it was already in me, every word. I know all the good stories. The one-eyed man and his talking donkey, the money in the catfish's mouth, the shepherd prince and his magical songs. Stories from the Book are the best stories there are.

Oh no, what time is it? I've messed around for too long. Gruff will be missing me. Someone will notice, Pugh or worse. They would kill Tommy if they found him, no question. They might even kill me too. All of a sudden I realize how dangerous this is, what I've gotten the both of us into.

"Will you take me to Aunt Barbara soon?" says Tommy. "I bet she's worried about me."

"Tommy, I got to go," I say. "I promise I'll be back later."

I run off toward camp as fast as I can go.

When I break the tree line all the boys are just waking up, cussing, hair sticking up with night sweat. Leebo cooking breakfast. The whole camp is in a groggy haze. I sneak up to Gruff's tent, but I don't have to check inside because I can hear him snoring from ten feet away.

I feel a small joy hopping in my chest. I got away with it. No one even noticed I was gone.

I spend an hour lounging, laughing with the boys, all of them still tired, all of them a little annoyed by me. I giggle and hop and sing, whatever I can to be noticed, to be as irritating as possible. I dance around Pugh so long I think he's going to smack me. Even sweet Leebo, head in his hands, eyes dark with rings around them, waves me off.

"Why don't you go out in the woods and run around for a while?" he says. "Nothing but old folks here, and not a one of us feeling much like fun."

I play it perfectly, and it couldn't go any better.

"Okay, Leebo," I say, and kiss him on the cheek.

He chuckles a little, then grabs his head and moans. Soon I'm back out in the forest, no problems from anyone. Even better, I bring presents. Nothing amazing, just a few things I could fit into my pack, a few things we had some extras of. Like a leather flap that John Gooding used to use as a tent, before he took off to the Northlands. Said he wanted to see what other places were like, what the ocean was. Said he wanted to off and see the whole world. I liked John Gooding. He was only six years older than me, and handsome too, except for his nose, which was crooked from a socking he took over some old lady. That's what he called her, his "old lady."

I also got a storybook—with pictures even, folks on camelback and great dunes rising high as palaces—and some leftover beans from last night. When I get back to the tree it's almost noon, and Tommy's waiting on me, not looking near as scared as last time. That means he's trusting me.

"Beans again?" says Tommy.

"Don't be ungrateful," I say. "Birds aren't ungrateful, and all they get is worms."

"But I don't want beans. They stink."

"Some birds don't even get worms. They get dead stuff. They don't even like food until it gets to stinking. You ever think about that?"

"Well, I ain't any bird."

"Nope," I say. "You're a growing boy, and as your very

own guardian angel, I say the Lord hath provided unto thee beans. So eat your durn beans."

"You don't have to get all huffy," he says. "I'm the one who got robbed by bandits. I'm the one trapped in the woods."

Trapped. I never thought of it like that. The woods are the only place I never felt trapped, the only place where I was free to go as I please. Not the town, not Templeton. You couldn't hardly step outside without fierce looks from the Townies, whispering from the kids and all the ladies, me and Momma walking heads high and proud, like she always told me to, from our house to the store and back again. If they whisper, it's because they're jealous, she always said. If they whisper, it's because you're more beautiful than they ever dreamed of being. If they whisper it's because we're the only ones who can heal their sick, who can magic all their dirt into flowers. Magic makes folks nervous, always has. People get scared of whatever they don't understand. Momma said it was a risk doing what she did, healing folks like that out in the open.

"Others wouldn't dare," said Momma.

"There are others?" I said.

Momma only smiled. She was always saying that kind of stuff, and I never hardly knew what she was talking about. But I walked proud, with my chin up, my eyes fixed at the clouds up above everybody's heads. Momma said the clouds were God's own handwriting, all the sky was, and the moon was what whispered the future to you. She said she could read mysteries in the way leaves fluttered and trees groaned in the wind, that all birds had their own song you could listen to like a ghost story. That they all had a point, that you could read them. She said she'd teach me one day, when I was good and ready.

I guess I didn't ever get good and ready enough. The only magic I know is the forgetting herbs. Well, that and the nothingsong. I always have the nothingsong.

But if I knew more magic like Momma did, I could show the woods to Tommy so that he would see them like I do. I could teach the woods to him, the wildness and birdsong, the way the trees hold the sunlight in them, all the way down to their roots. Then he wouldn't feel trapped anymore. He'd feel freer than he ever did in any grubby old town anyway.

In the corner of my mind I see the Preacher lurking. His shadow, the hat and hair wild as fire sparking out from under it, the long tear-trail of a scar down his cheek. His hands reach out at me, fingers grasping.

"Whatcha thinking about?" says Tommy. "You got that look like a wiped-off dish. You look like an empty plate."

"Finish your beans," I say.

I snap a twig with my fingers just to hear it break.

The night passes about the same, Tommy and I huddled close in the dark under the tree. We don't start that way, we start ten feet apart and slowly he scoots toward me till we both wake up tangled together and sweating in the morning sunlight. After that I sneak off and go wander around camp, chirping at everybody till they tell me to go away again. I even poke my head in the war tent, just to be a nuisance. Gruff and awful old Pugh are huddled over a map, talking something serious. I better bug them.

"Whatcha talking about, Gruff?"

Gruff shakes his head at me and says, "Goldeline, love of my heart, can't you go and bother Leebo or somebody? Help Dunce with the dishes. I don't care. Just get useful, and get out of my hair."

Normally that would hurt my feelings a little for Gruff to talk to me like that, but this time I planned it so it's okay. He's been awful grumpy lately though.

"Anything I can help you with, Gruff?" I say.

"Not unless you can kill the Preacher for us," snaps Pugh.

I stop cold. "The Preacher?"

"Yes, the Preacher," says Pugh. "That crazy-haired tyrant running town to town, warning everybody about us, making everyone follow him or die."

"Cool it, Pugh," says Gruff.

"The Preacher can't get us here," I say. "We're safe in the woods."

"Not yet he can't," says Pugh. "But he'll come for us, just you wait. One of those Townie cowards will tip him off about us and he'll come and snap our necks and set us on fire, cook us up real good, same as he did to your momma."

Gruff slaps Pugh so hard it knocks him into the dirt.

"I said to cool it, Pugh," says Gruff. "You gonna shut up now?"

"The Preacher won't get me, will he?" I say.

"No, darlin'," says Gruff.

"You promise?" I say.

"I promise," he says. "Now get out of the war tent. You know better than to come in here."

"Sorry, Gruff," I say.

As I'm leaving I hear him tell Pugh to get on up, what was he thinking, if Gruff ever catches him talking about my momma that way again he'll fix him good. I hate Pugh. I hope he trips and busts his head somewhere.

But the Preacher I'm scared of. I have dreams sometimes, his wild white hair, the scar under his eye, his fingers spread wide and twitching the air like a spell caster, like an evil magician. All the Townies with their dumb faces looking up at the Preacher, believing every evil word he spits. He scares me in my dreams.

I head out to the woods, and soon I'm back with Tommy. His face is dirty and his clothes have blood on them from tramping around through briars. He's starting to stink too. I figure if I'm pretending to be his guardian angel I might as well go all out and take care of him.

"Shoot, Tommy," I say. "Smells like someone needs a bath."

"Aw, come on. I hate baths."

"You ever had a creek bath before?" I say.

"You mean with fish and frogs and worms? Heck no. Momma always bathed me in a tub, like you're supposed to."

"Not anymore," I say. "The creek is your bathtub. This whole forest is full of stuff you can bathe in."

"Savages and poor folks are the only people who go muck around in creeks and rivers and all that."

"Guess what? You're both of those things now. Savage and poor. Come on, we ain't got all day."

I lead him through the thicket, down a little deer path I found one day out wandering. It goes to this tiny creek I don't think anybody knows about, except maybe some ghosts. It's hard to see ghosts in a town, where most folks either don't believe in them or just would rather not think about it one way or the other. But Momma believed in ghosts, and she taught me how to be quiet and listen for them. The woods are the best place for ghosts, like it's here they feel most free to show up. I saw a beautiful pale woman drink fire from the creek one night, and I heard a little baby wailing in the dark where no one was. But I've never seen a breathing person here.

We pass a bunch of redbud trees in full bloom, which are my favorite because they aren't red at all, they're bright sunset purple, like a trader woman's scarf. Tommy doesn't see any of it though. He's just arms crossed, huffing along like I'm leading him on to his death.

"Perk up," I say. "It's just a stupid bath, Tommy."

"It's a bath with a bunch of dirty things."

"Well, you're right about that. But you ever seen a dirty fish?"

"Yeah I have. I seen plenty of dirty fish at the market. Dirty fish, and they stink and got flies all over them."

"But you ever seen a dirty fish in a river?" I say.

Tommy stops to think about it. He puts a freckly finger to his lip.

"No, I guess not. I guess I never have."

"Nothing cleaner in the world than a river fish. They don't start to stink till they get caught. Now I'm about to bathe you in free water."

We break the tree line and come to the creek. It isn't much, no river or anything, but it pools up just a little bit upstream, into a baby-type waterfall. There's always a snake or two, but if you're loud and let them know you're coming and don't spook them, then you're fine. I take a stick and bash the water around with it.

"We're coming, snakes!" I say. "Don't you get scared."

"Snakes?" says Tommy.

"Oh, hush up. It's just a formality."

"A what?"

"Nothing. Lookee, we're here."

The creek really is something beautiful. The zigzaggy waterfall, the pool at the bottom, the rock floor where you can even see your toes it's so clean. Not a lot of creeks like that around here. Most are dirty, the color of runny dump. But this creek is my creek. It's special. I haven't thought of a good name for it yet.

"See? I told you this creek was something else," I say. "It might be the most magical place in the whole woods."

"I don't believe in magic," says Tommy. "That's just kids' stuff."

"But you believe in angels?"

"Of course I do," he says. "You're standing right there, aren't you?"

"I am," I say, "but you can only see me because I let you. The whole world's chock-full of things you can't see. They're all around you, whether you believe in them or not. Now get on in that water already, we ain't got all day."

While Tommy bathes, I turn around and gander off at a dogwood tree, the little bloody drops on its flowers. There's an old story about dogwoods, how one time a dogwood tree held a man who was in such great pain that it stained the blossoms forever. That's a flower story I can understand, even if it's just made up. Maybe even the dogwood tree knows it's made up and plays along anyway. You got to like a tree who will do something like that.

Yeah, or maybe the tree really believes it, and that's what makes its flowers so pretty. Can faith make you pretty? Or is it just being a sucker? I listen to Tommy splash around in the water, giggling to himself, and I'm thinking that this kid is the most gullible person I ever met. I mean, I told him I was an angel and he actually believed me. You don't get much more gullible than that. But maybe that's something good about him. Maybe that means I got to protect him.

Speaking of, I got to get back to camp soon, lest Gruff or somebody starts missing me.

"Hurry it up, will you?" I holler.

"Why? The water's nice," he says. "And there's a turtle over there."

"Because I got angel stuff to do. I can't just sit here all day while you float around, pointing out the wildlife."

"What kind of angel stuff?"

I keep my back to him, but I'm starting to get mad.

"The kind that'll flat burn your ears out if I told you," I say. "Now if you don't get out of that water this second, I'm dragging you out by your neck, you hear me?"

Walking back to our tree, Tommy won't even look at me.

"Aw, come on," I say. "What's the matter?"

"You're mean for an angel," he says. "And where are you always sneaking off to? Where do you get the food and all that?"

"Don't you remember what happens in the Book any time an angel shows up? Everyone gets scared. They hit the dirt they're quaking so bad. I got on my girl suit right now because otherwise I'd straight scare the hellfire from you. You wouldn't even be able to look at me. You'd fall down and try to worship me, same as everyone else in the Book."

"Worship you?" he says. "Fat chance."

I turn to him with my fiercest angel scowl, as much mean and Gruff as I can summon. "What did you say to me?"

"Nothing."

The kid's shaking all over. I hate to spook him like that, but hopefully it scared him out of asking me any more questions. I don't know how long I can keep up this angel business. I don't know why I started it in the first place. It seemed like a game, I guess. But it'll be bad news if Tommy ever figures it out.

"Now you stay put," I say. "I'm going to go get you some grub."

"Can't I come with you?" he says. "I'm sick of sitting around here, waiting."

"Didn't I already tell you about angel business?" I say.

"Fine," he says.

I head back into the trees. But before I get too far I stop and turn back to Tommy. He's sitting there on the ground, picking his nose. He's such easy prey for anything that comes along, bear or bandit. Or Preacher. A cloud blocks the little bit of sunlight that would come through the trees, and the woods around me darken. *Something is out there*, says the little voice in me. *Something is coming for you, Goldeline. For you and Tommy both.*

I shake my head and the cloud moves and the sunlight sprinkles back through the branches in little bars of gold. Nothing is out there. No Preacher, with his wild hair and scar down his cheek. He's not out there, not carrying a torch and a knife, not sneaking up on me from the darkest corner of my dreams. It's just woods stuff. Nothing is hunting me. I go on my way back to the camp.

FOUR

For dinner Leebo cooks up a stew. It smells bad, but it'll do. I fill my bowl up a second time for Tommy.

"Hungry there?" says Pugh. He's standing right behind me and I didn't even notice him, I'm so worried about this Tommy stuff. I got to be more careful or I'll ruin everything.

"Starved," I say.

"You're gonna get fat, the way you been eating lately," he says.

"What are you even talking about, Pugh?"

"I seen you take an extra bowl last night too. I seen you taking extra the last few days." He smiles. "And that's Mr. Pugh to you."

I don't know what to say. I don't have any excuses.

"Come on now, Pugh," says Leebo. "She's a growing girl,

ain't she? Grew half a foot just since last year. It makes a body awful hungry to be growing all the time."

"She's got a secret," says Pugh. "Little minx is up to something."

"You don't talk about Miss Goldeline that way," says Leebo. "You got a nasty mind, Pugh. Plain mean."

"You'll see," says Pugh. "Before long I'll show all of you. Never should have picked the girl up in the first place. She'll be the ruin of us, mark my words." He squints his evil eye at me. "I'm watching you, girlie. One mess-up and I'll be there." Pugh puts a hand to his knife, a curved fang of a weapon. "I won't let you mess up twice."

When he walks away I realize my hands are shaking. If it wasn't for Leebo that could have gotten much worse.

"Ignore the cranky old sod." Leebo chuckles. "You're a smart one, you are. A good girl. I know you wouldn't ever do anything to hurt Gruff and all us boys out here. Ain't that right?"

"Sure thing, Leebo," I say, and give him my best smile.

Stupid. I got to be more careful. I already kept Tommy safe, kept him from forgetting, from being lost and wandering out in the woods. He knows that we're bandits out here and not ghosts—that it's real human bandits who can be caught and killed. Sure, the Preacher might suspect it, but regular old folks like Tommy are still scared, and that fear protects us. How do I keep Tommy safe and not be the death of Gruff and all the boys? How do I keep everyone from dying, much less protect myself? Pugh would kill me if he knew about Tommy, and I bet not even Gruff would stop him. I would deserve getting killed. I got everyone's lives depending on me, and not a one of them knows it. What would they say if they knew? It's a dangerous game I'm playing, and I don't even know what in the heck I'm playing it for.

I take a deep breath and walk my way back into the forest, Tommy's momma's dress dragging in the dirt behind me.

Come nightfall me and Tommy are lying together, up under the tree. We got rocks for pillows and the ground is cool and soft. Fuzzy finger-long caterpillars tremble over my arms with their clown faces. The moon's just a wink in the sky and the stars are a warm happy sigh. An owl up in the tree keeps looking over its shoulder. All you mice out there better buck up and hide. Owl's gone hunting. And he hoots like he hears me the whole time. Maybe he does.

My momma could talk to animals. We had a cat named Marybell and she and Momma would purr back and forth at each other for hours. I've seen birds land on her sweet shoulder and the way the fish would swarm around her feet when we bathed in the river. The sun would hit their scales and they'd turn into treasure. I would chase and never catch them, little ghosts of gold that flitted away downstream, that were never mine to have. They were the river's own money, Momma said, and we should let them be.

"Were you ever a human girl?" Tommy says. "A normal girl and not just an angel?"

I was a normal girl with Momma. I was just any other little kid when Momma was still alive, before the Preacher came for us.

"Yep," I say. "Once, a long long time ago."

"How did you die?"

Suddenly there's eyes looking down at me everywhere. Bats in the trees, owls out in the night, bugs out from under the rocks. Even the stars are staring. There's a tree that looks like an old lady stirring a pot, and her leaves bend down to listen. I can't lie, not with all these witnesses, not with the whole of heaven and nature breathing down my neck. So I take a deep breath and I say it.

"When my momma got burned up, they burned me up too. That's when I died and became an angel."

"Don't only witches and heretics get burned?"

"Not when it's heretics done the burning."

"Oh," he says. "My momma died too."

"I know, Tommy."

"It's not fair that mommas have to die. I'd be dead too if I didn't have you. I wouldn't even be here anymore. I'd be gone."

"But you aren't gone. You're here and so am I and so is the moon. We're okay."

"What is heaven like?"

I got to think real hard about this. I got to get this just right.

"Heaven is like a big warm bed, with fresh white sheets that smell like honeysuckle. Heaven is a table full of food and everyone you love is sitting right there. And they don't got wrinkles except from laughing and they're just how you remember them, not even how they really were. It's the table where you really belong, really truly finally belong, like home. And everyone talks like singing birds. Every time anyone opens their mouths it's nothing but a song."

"And that's where my momma is right now?"

"She's up there, chowing down. She's sitting next to God and your daddy and they're waving down at you right now."

"That sounds nice. That sounds real nice."

Soon Tommy's sleeping, the softest snores you ever heard. The owl takes off, his great wide wings cutting through the night quiet. I'm glad Tommy's asleep. Any more talk about heaven and my heart would have busted open and all my rivers come rolling out. I never told anyone about my momma before that didn't already know. I never talked about it to anyone except Gruff. I know I'm just tricking Tommy but I don't want him to leave. Not yet.

I got to figure a way to tell him the truth about me. I got to figure a way to keep him.

Morning comes quick and I'm up with the dew. I sneak off early because I want to surprise Tommy. I could cook him some cornbread, maybe pick out a new book. There's all kinds of treasures that Gruff didn't think we could sell or trade. Maybe I can find something for Tommy, something to cheer him up. Everyone likes presents.

The morning is smiling on me. Even the fog seems happy, like wrapping paper for me to tear through and find the day. A red fox yawns and sniffs the air. When it sees me, I wave and it bolts, off and gone into nothing. It's a gift though, because I never see foxes, not here. The morning birds holler and a woodpecker smashes its beak into something far off. The woods isn't just the trees, it's a million leaves flinging dew to the breeze, the buzz of horseflies and honeybees, the grumble of worms under my feet. It's like a song that nobody has ears big enough to make sense of, like a song God wrote just for Himself.

I break the tree line into camp with my head full of music. I can see the boys all waking up in the distance, just out of earshot. Leebo's stoking the fire, ready for breakfast, and Gruff stretches himself in the long velvet robe, coming out of his tent like a lion from a den.

I raise my hand to wave at him when there's a snap of

twigs behind me, back in the woods. I turn around, and not twenty feet from me he stands, redheaded, bug-eyed, scared out of his mind. Tommy. He followed me. I guess I had my head so stuffed with everything good I didn't even have the sense to listen for him. No wonder the fox left me so fast. I been dreading this, even though I knew it had to happen, same as every bad thing in the world. Tommy tries to run but I'm faster than him.

I tackle Tommy and pin him down. He's crying so hard he can barely talk. It's all over. I knew I was too happy. You can't ever let yourself get too happy. That's when bad stuff comes. That's when everything goes the most wrong.

"You're one of them," Tommy says. "One of the bad guys."

"They're not bad."

"They robbed us. They sent Miss Lyons off into the woods."

"They saved my life and here I am, saving yours."

"You can't be both bad and good. You're one or the other."

"That's not true," I say. "It isn't so simple as that."

"Get off me."

"Only if you won't run."

When I get up, he takes off running. I catch him pretty quick and sling him into the leaves. I put both my knees on his chest and sit there so he can't move.

"Where are you gonna run, Tommy? You don't know how to get back to the road. You're stuck here unless I help you."

"You told me you were an angel. You wear my momma's dress. You lied to me. You're a wicked girl, bad right down to your toes."

He's right. I'm about the worst thing there is.

"All I wanted was a friend," I say, and I realize it's true.

"You'll never be any friend of mine," he says, crying.

I don't know what to do. I can't turn him into Gruff and them, much less Pugh. They'll kill him, and maybe even me. Only thing I can do is let him go. I got to trust Tommy like I never trusted anybody except Momma in my life.

"Get up," I say. "I'll take you to the road. I will. Just promise me you won't tell anybody we're here. Tell them you got lost."

"First thing I do is go to the sheriff. I'll have all them bandits hanged."

Growling in my best Gruff voice, I say, "You say one word to the sheriff and I'll slit your throat. I don't care where you run off to, where you hide. I'll find you and I'll kill you dead."

Tommy starts bawling again. I crawl off him and crouch in front of him.

"Listen. I will take you to the road. Just shut up and follow me."

He shakes my hand off when I try to help him up. The kid won't even look at me. My friend. I messed this one up about as bad as I could have messed anything. I ruined it. I ruined it forever. It was so good to have a friend. I never knew how alone I had been until I finally wasn't anymore. I'm so scared it can't be fixed, that I messed up for real. One mess-up can last forever if it's bad enough, like selling your soul to the Evil One. There's all kinds of unforgivable sins. That's how life is.

It's a long, sad walk. When we get to the road I point the way to the nearest town, to Templeton, where all the Townies are. I wish I could tell him to go somewhere else, but the other towns are too far away. Tommy would never make it alone.

"You'll be able to find a way home from there," I say. "Please don't tell anybody about us. They'll kill me."

Tommy still won't look at me, won't answer either. He starts off slow down the road.

"Tommy?"

He stops but doesn't turn.

"I'm gonna miss you. You were the only friend I ever had."

"Liar," Tommy says, and takes off running. He's limping a little, like when I tackled him he got hurt. I watch him hobble, red hair and all, down the road until it bends and he's gone.

It's the worst day I can remember. It's the worst day since Momma died.

When it's nighttime I go to Gruff's tent and poke my head in and ask if he'll come out and sit with me a moment.

"Come on, Goldy," he says. "I'm worn slap out. How about we just talk over breakfast? Maybe Leebo can fry us up some eggs or something. It'll be a treat."

"Please?" I say. "Just for a minute."

I give him my best poor pitiful orphan face. As tough as he acts, that kind of thing never fails with Gruff.

"Fine, fine," he says. "I'll come out and sit with ye. Hold on a second while I collect myself."

Pretty soon Gruff comes huffing out of his tent. I've got my back up against a great big oak tree, watching the stars hang their fire in its branches. The trunk is wide enough for two to lean back on, if they don't mind bumping shoulders, and Gruff sits down to join me.

I lay my head on Gruff's shoulder, like he is the daddy I never had. He smells like wine and sweat and dirt. He smells like fish and blood and rusty old swords. He smells like fairy books and ancient legends in torn old stolen bloody books. He smells like Moon Haven does in my dreams, the place I always want to go, the place I pray one day will be my home. I hear a noise outside, a chattering up in the trees, maybe bats invisible over our heads, but I don't mind bats, lonely hanging things that don't bother anyone, blind hunters in the dark.

"I love you, Gruff," I say. "You're my only person in the world now."

"The heck are you talking like that for?"

I'm crying a little. I can feel the hot running down my cheeks. I hate to cry in front of Gruff, but I can't help it.

"You love me too, right?"

"Well, yeah, I love you, Goldeline," he says, a little embarrassed by my tears. "You're like my own daughter. Never thought I'd have kids, seeing as how I'm not much of the poppa type. But if I had to have one, I'm glad it wound up being you."

"You think I'm a real bandit yet?"

"I'd say you're an almost-bandit," he says, chuckling. "I'd say you're about as near to a real bandit as a kid can be."

"Is that enough to get me into Moon Haven?"

"When we go to Moon Haven, you and me, they'll let us in just fine. They'll throw a durn parade for us is what they'll do. By then you'll be a real bandit, one hundred percent."

"Good," I say.

The crickets scratch themselves and give us their song. I sing a little too, in my heart, a quiet nothingsong, a comfort one. Gruff pats me on my head.

"Come on, let's get some sleep," he says. "We got us a busy day tomorrow. Got to pack up the camp again, find somewhere else to hide ourselves. Always got to stay on the move, always on the run. It's the bandits' life, you know?"

"Just another minute," I say, trying to keep my voice steady.

"Whatever you say, Goldy." Gruff yawns, big and lionlike.

"Though if we keep sitting here, I'm liable to fall asleep. Wake up bit all over with mosquitoes."

No way I'm falling asleep. Not here with Gruff, under the sky and planets and stars.

"Hey, Gruff?"

"Mmhmm?" he says, eyes shut, arms crossed around himself.

I got to tell him. He's so good to me, and I put him and all of us in such danger. I'm so stupid. I got to be brave and tell him, no matter what happens.

"I might have done something bad," I say.

But Gruff's already asleep. He's snoring, his mustache quavers with it. I go inside his tent and grab his blanket, spread it over him as best I can.

I hope I've done right. I hope what I did won't ruin it all. I hope I didn't sin by letting Tommy go. At least we're moving the camp tomorrow. That gives me some peace. At least everyone will be safe after that. For a while, anyway.

I go to my little tent and try to sleep for a few hours, but it's no good. I creep back outside, the full red moon glowing like an ember, enough light to pass for haunted day, shimmering and fairy-blessed. Momma believed in fairies, though she said you'd never see them. She would call them up sometimes, ask for things. They'd answer by the whispering of the leaves, by a rustle in the bushes or the howl of a wolf. Momma could hear. She was magic and could understand. All fairy talk ever sounded like to me was normal old nature. Momma said I would grow into it, that one day I could talk to invisible things too, that I could hear them and understand. Sometimes the fairies would leave us gifts on our doorstep—a pile of acorns, a pair of daisy chains for Momma and me to wear as crowns. Tonight the moonlight is gift enough.

I wish Momma were here.

FIVE

That night, asleep in my tent, I have the dream. It's the same one as always, it starts the same way. I'm littler, and it's Momma's trial. Me and all the people of the village are gathered at the town square. The day is dark and smeary, hot as bad breath. Momma's in the town square up on the scaffolding the Preacher had built, her white hair long down her back, all the fierce she's got in her eyes. I can tell she's scared, I can see her tremble a little in her knees. But my momma holds her head up straight, even though the Preacher calls her devil to her face, even though the Townies spit and shout horrors at her. This is the end, and my momma looks beautiful.

A cardinal posts up on a pole next to her, and Momma keeps looking over to it like she's asking for help. The

Preacher's in his black suit, same one he always has, with that phony gleaming sheriff's badge on his chest. He stands up on the scaffolding with Momma, like it's a stage. This way he can be above all of us. This way we can all see.

I'm in the crowd, after Momma cut my hair off, wearing Momma's shawl so no one knows it's me. Momma told me to run but I didn't know where to run off to. And I have to see her. I can't leave her alone.

"I never done anything folks didn't ask me to," she says. "They all know what I am, and I've never done a thing but help the people here."

The Preacher spits in disgust.

"Liar," he says. "Is it not true that you have held congress with the Evil One?"

"I never met any devils," Momma says, "much less anybody so grand or wicked as the Evil One. Unless of course you see the Evil One up here, staring me right in the face."

"You heard it yourself!" says the Preacher. "You heard her say she spoke with the Evil One himself!"

He dances around on his platform, waving his arms wild, while storm clouds rumble behind him. A soft rain begins.

"They have witches up in the Northlands too, you know that?" he says. "Up in the Northlands where they're brave enough to drive witchcraft out from their midst. Does the Book not say, 'A witch shall be known by her deeds, and by her deeds she shall be condemned'?"

The Preacher is tall, balding a little bit on his forehead, with long white hair in the back, but handsome in the way that makes you catch your breath, even if you hate him. His right eye is bluer than the left, like a frosty windowpane in winter, and he's got a long scar down his cheek. The Townie women all used to say how good-looking he was, especially before he got his scar, before he left for all those years, how he would have made a good husband. Momma's hands are tied behind her back. The Preacher points at her.

"Pretty, isn't she?" he says, his words weaving like a spider's web through the air, a string of invisible magic spread out over the crowd, poisoning every ear that hears. "But her heart is a deep pit, a well of brackish water, and she has infected this community long enough."

The crowd jeers, flings garbage and rotten food at Momma. But she refuses to cry, she refuses to bow her head.

"You used to be such a sweet man," says Momma. "What happened to you, Cyrus? Where did you go?"

I never know why Momma says that. I never know why she calls him Cyrus.

The Preacher grabs a torch from one of the Townies. He lifts it on high like a king's scepter. The flame casts a golden flicker on Momma's face.

"You did this," he says to Momma. "Nobody but you."

Momma doesn't scream though, she doesn't cry. Not through the accusations, not through the hours of questions.

Not once. Not until she sees me.

I don't mean for her to. But she does. I got up too close and she picked me out, even under the hood and everything. Her chin quivers and I can see her start shaking. I know that just by being here and seeing all this, I'm breaking her heart.

The cardinal flies off from the pole. The whole town goes silent.

I scream.

Now is the part in the dream where Gruff claps his hand over my mouth. When he whispers, *Come with me, Goldy. Come out to the woods with me.* It's my favorite part, the only good in the whole dream, where Gruff calls me princess, his Goldy, his sunflower. Found myself some men, he says. The old rabblers from the tavern. Gruff says the town is getting too religious, says this new religion is giving him the creeps. Time to head off somehow. Where we going, Gruff? Somewhere. And he carries me off to the woods.

"But what about Momma?" I ask him, when we're good and far away, hidden deep in the forest. "When is Momma coming to meet us?"

Gruff grabs me then by the shoulders, softly but firm, and he stares me right in the eyes in a way that lets me know that I can trust him, that no matter how awful it is he will always tell me the truth.

"Your momma is gone, Goldeline," he says.

And I cry and I cry and Gruff holds me, and he whispers

that always he will take care of me, that he will keep me safe. Shh, Goldeline, cry it on out, Gruff is here for you, Gruff will always be here for you.

That's how it always happens.

But this time, in the dream, Gruff isn't there. This time when hands grab me it's the Preacher. Somehow he's vanished off the platform and he's behind me, he's got his hands over my mouth. Suddenly it's not just him that's the Preacher, all the Townies are preachers, every last one of them dressed up just like him, with a great black hat like his, with teeth filed down like knives.

Then I wake up.

SIX

I sit up in my tent, terrified. Something's wrong, I know it. Something awful has happened. I can feel it all over me like fever sweat.

But when I run out into the sunlight, all seems well. I slept late. Judging by the sun, it's almost ten. That's okay, everyone seems to be a slow riser today anyhow. The boys are taking their time with the pack-up, wore out and tired of moving all the time. Leebo stokes the fire. Gruff stretches out. One of the boys is still passed out down by the fire. There's a gray line of cloud off in the distance, like rain is coming soon.

A cat walks up to me, a long, slinking orange thing. It licks its paw and stares up at me, one ear missing a chunk, like it got in a fight or something.

"What secret do you know, kitty cat?" I say.

A cardinal lands on a twig above me, its little harp song short and scared. Then comes another. It lands on the same branch, and they whistle at me. Two more, three, like a speckle of blood drops dripping from the tree limbs. I've never seen so many in one place before, such pretty birds. They take flight all at once, a big red heart that hangs in the sky a moment before vanishing off into the woods. It's beautiful.

Something snaps like a twig in my heart, and I know it's too late.

They come through the trees dressed in black, with long black cloaks dragging like shadows. Like giant wicked spiders they come sneaking out of the woods. Tall men, short men, some Townies and some not. Their faces stern and grimacing. They have knives, they have guns, they're all around us. At least a dozen men. I see them first.

"Gruff!" I scream.

But they're already coming. The boys aren't ready. Most of them are still half asleep, or messing with the tents. I scream and I scream and I scream. They're all over Gruff's boys like maggots, men in black cloaks all alike streaming from the forest, a deranged army of them. The taller men have torches, they set the tents on fire. I can't do anything to fix it. I can only stand here and watch.

Leebo drops the stew and gets moving on his crutch,

headed for the woods. Gruff ducks a shot and it shatters a tree limb behind him. I want to run to him, but there are men in cloaks, six at least, between us. I know I'd never make it.

"Goldy!" he hollers. "Get out of here!"

"I can't leave you," I say.

"Don't you worry about me," he says. "Come find me. You know where. I'll be waiting on you."

And I do. I know exactly where to go.

I take one more look back toward Gruff and drop to my belly. I crawl my way to the trees until the sounds of rifles and men screaming seem far away. When I get up to run something hits me in the head and I fall flat. I roll over and one-eyed Pugh stands over me. He's got his knife out, the long, fanged one.

"You did this," he says. "I knew you were up to something. I knew it all along. See, Gruff trusted you, but I didn't. And now I'm gonna make you suffer."

Another shot fires so loud it hurts my ears and Pugh slumps over on top of me. I try to push him off, but Pugh's body is too heavy, I can't move him. I hear a pistol cock and I figure I'm done for.

"Wait," a voice says. "We're supposed to get her alive. Boss said so."

I'm yanked off the ground by my shoulders. I bite the man's wrist and I kick and he drops me. He's a Townie. I've seen him. These are Templeton men. I growl at him.

"Easy now," he says.

I jump at him like a wolf girl. I want to bite his throat off. Another man whacks me with the butt of his gun and my face hits the dirt.

"She's a demon," says the Townie. He's got blond hair in a ponytail. I think he is a lawyer back in Templeton.

"Boss says to take her. He promised the kid. They made a deal."

The kid? Does he mean Tommy?

They tie my hands with rope. I kick and I fight but they're too strong for me. One of them, a huge man, slaps me so hard I wonder if I haven't lost a tooth. I wonder if I got one less fang to fix on his throat when he lets me go.

"He didn't say we couldn't do that," he says, and they both laugh.

Behind me I hear gunfire, and I'm scared for all Gruff's boys. When people die they just become dog food, spoiled meat for scavengers, bones for the grass to swallow. It doesn't matter that you love them. Love doesn't do anybody any good, it can't protect you from a bullet or a knife, it can't keep you from just becoming a body. I hope some of Gruff's boys made it free to the woods. I hope anyone escaped. But mostly what I don't see is Gruff, and my heart goes soft for a second. He's not dead or captured. He got away. And as soon as I can get out of here, I'm going to go and meet him.

The two men drag me, hands behind my back, pulling me back into their world, their town, and no one I love left to fight it with. Around me the birds and bugs call my name, the whir of mosquitoes in the coming dark of a storm, the sad fury of faraway lightning. Off we go toward the main road, where God knows what terror is right there waiting on me.

SEVEN

The men bash through the path, hacking and tearing, ripping a highway through my quiet, secret trail. They drag me through the dirt behind them. I kick and fight and make them earn every inch.

"You sure we can't just kill her?" says the blond one.

"Nuh-uh. Our orders are pretty dang clear."

What orders? Did Tommy rat on me? Is all of this his fault?

The blond-headed one is stupid. I think maybe I could scare him.

"If you don't let me go, I'll curse you," I say.

"That a fact? What you gonna do, spit on me?"

"I'll make spiders lay eggs in your nose. I'll have hornets sting your tongue. You'll spend every morning pulling leeches off your eyelids forever."

"Whoa now. Little brat got her a mouth, don't she?"

The huge guy picks me up and I kick as hard as I can. Then he drops me. I land on my face. It hurts.

"Now shut up and get a move on."

When we make it to the road they bring me up to a big black carriage. They open the door and toss me in and there's Tommy.

That's how they found us. I knew I did wrong keeping him safe, I knew it. And Tommy led them here, to Gruff's camp. The men dead or captured, and it's because of Tommy. It's because of me.

"Don't put her in here!" Tommy screams. "Not with me!"

I jump on him and bite the first thing I can get to. It's his thumb. I make good and sure I draw blood. The blond-headed man pulls me off Tommy.

"You little heathen," he says. "Behave or you'll wind up in the ditch with the other degenerates."

He shuts the carriage door and leaves me face-to-face with Tommy.

Tommy's hair looks redder, and his eyes bluer, and somehow he looks older, like being with me grew him up a little. He holds his bleeding thumb under his arm, and his eyes are full of tears. I take a deep breath and he flinches, like he knows that I could rip him in half if I wanted to. But there's this other feeling too, this weird one where I'm a little bit glad to see him. Like I have my friend back. Then I remember how I've lost everything again and I hate Tommy even more.

"They're all dead," I say. "They got them all."

Except Gruff, but I keep quiet about that.

"Good thing too," Tommy says. His voice shakes, but he's not just scared. He's angry too. His cheeks go red with it and he cries a little. "They deserved it. You better be glad I let you off easy."

"They were all I had," I say.

"You lied to me," says Tommy. "You told me you were an angel." He wipes his nose on his shirtsleeve. "I was scared when they found me, all lost on the road. Just some men in a carriage going slow through the woods. They picked me up and gave me some food. They asked me what happened and I told them, about how we were ambushed, how bandits robbed us, how the driver and poor Miss Lyons were off lost and starving somewhere. I told them every word. I said I got an aunt Barbara and would they take me to her and they said okay, but first you got to show us where the bandits are. I said okay but they have a little girl with them and you have to protect the girl. I made them promise before I showed them. They said okay so I took them to the trail, I showed them right where it started and I said follow it. I could have had them kill you but I didn't. It's my fault you're still alive. So we're even."

I got a few more words for Tommy, but not now. Now I got to get out of here. So I think about Gruff and I make myself mean and tough again. I squint and build a fire inside myself, a roaring, smoking thing, the sort that swallows houses and woods and whole towns. Once it's big and stoking, I growl back at Tommy.

"Like heck we're even. They're going to take me back to Templeton and burn me up, same as they did my momma. At best they'll put me in jail. Nothing good comes to me after this."

"Well, I don't know what you expect me to do about it," says Tommy. "You better be happy you're still alive."

Tommy's crying big and real now. I almost got him.

"I'll tell you what you can do about it," I say. "You can let me loose."

"Nope. No way."

"Just untie my hands. I'll sneak out. No one will know it was you."

"Who the heck else would it be?" he says.

"Tell them I'm a witch. Tell them I conjured the knots open. Tell them I bit your finger so hard you thought it was gonna fall off. I don't give a care what you tell them, just let me go."

That scares him a little, I can tell. He's covering himself like he thinks I might actually do it.

"All right, all right. But then you better go. I better not

ever see you again ever."

"Cross my heart, slice my tongue, sew my eyeballs shut, never will you ever. Now get the durn ropes off me."

Tommy gets to fumbling with the knots when I hear a voice that makes my stomach fall, that makes my blood go quiet. It's one I remember from my dreams, full and gravelly, one that shivers my spine. Tommy finally unties the ropes.

"There. You happy now?"

"Hush up."

A light rain prattles on the roof of the carriage. I ease the door open a little and take a peek. Just as quick I pull my head back in, my whole body gone grave-cold, the voice like a shadow down inside me.

The man stands as tall as in my nightmares.

The white hair wild under his wide-brimmed black hat, eyes blue as a far-off lake, the draggled scar down his cheek.

The man in every bad dream I ever had, the silvery voice that slithers into my ears, that wakes me up screaming at night. The wicked man, the vicious man, cruel and horrible. The man who took everything I ever had from me.

I have dreaded this day, Momma, I prayed it would never come.

It's him. The Preacher.

"What's the matter?" says Tommy.

My hands and feet are numb. I feel invisible ants crawl over my body. I'm dizzy. It's that day all over again, the one from my dream. Only this time I'm captured and Gruff has run off and I have no one and I'm alone in the world. I'm alone and it's my fault.

"You look like you're sick," says Tommy. "You gonna puke in here?"

I hold my finger up to my lips and Tommy gets it now. He gets that I'm scared. I sneak out lightly, hoping my bare feet and the rain will keep me from being heard. The Preacher's off talking to the blond-headed man who caught me, so now is my chance. My heart knows that I am in great danger and I have to hurry.

I only make it about ten steps before he stops me cold. It's his voice, rich and full and deep, like your bones hear it even before your ears do.

"What do we have here?"

I'm afraid to turn around. I'm afraid to look into his face. His fingers graze my hair and I shiver all over.

"You look just like your mother."

I can't let him know how much I love to hear that. I can't let the Preacher know how proud that makes me in my heart.

"My momma's dead," I say. "She was a baker over in Rawlingsville. You got to be mistaken."

I don't dare look up at him. I can't look past my feet. I let my hair dangle over my eyes so he can't tell I'm crying.

"I knew it was you," says the Preacher. "The second that little boy said there was a girl in the woods with them I knew it had to be you. I knew it had to be her daughter." I glance up at him real fast and I catch his eyes. A smile slides like a snake across his face. "I knew it had to be her daughter causing all this horror. Nobody but one of hers could stir up so much fear and devilment."

I try to talk high and unscared. I try to sound as little-girly as I can.

"I don't know what you're talking about, mister."

But I know he can hear it. I know he knows how scared I am.

"You don't remember me, do you?" says the Preacher.

"I remember you plenty," I say, my voice gone fierce. "You burned Momma. You're the Preacher."

The blond-headed man grabs at me, but he slips in the mud. I hop on his back and pull the knife out of his belt scabbard. I wave it out in front of me like I know what to do with it.

"Don't you lay a finger on me," I growl in my best Gruff voice, "lest you plan on losing it."

The Preacher laughs. He snatches at me and I swing at his hands and miss and he's giggling he's so happy.

"No, I don't think you do remember me. Not quite. But I remember you, Goldeline," he says.

How does the Preacher know my name?

Lightning cracks up above us and the animals scatter to the deeper parts of the trees. The rain falls in giant strings straight from heaven and the lightning rips the sky like angel veins. The Preacher lunges at me and my back is to the carriage and I don't know what to do. But then I remember Tommy, and I open the carriage door and yank him out into the mud. I pull him up by his hair and hold the knife to his throat.

"Take one step closer to me," I growl, "and I'm opening this kid up."

The Preacher may be wicked, but he's still a preacher. Tommy's just a kid, an innocent, a victim, and it doesn't do for the Preacher to spill his blood in front of all these people just to capture me. I know he won't let that happen. The Preacher folds his arms and smiles at me, his hair gone wet and limp and clinging to him where he looks like some rain-soaked death just crawled up out from the river. The huge man takes a step toward me and I needle Tommy's neck with the knife.

Tommy screams and I whisper *Sorry* in his ear so quiet not even a bird could hear it.

"Now don't you come after me," I say. "Don't you take one step toward us."

I know I'm backing the wrong way from the road. I'm not going toward camp. The camp is ruined, Gruff is gone, all his boys are gone or scattered. I can't go back there. It doesn't even exist anymore. It's dead and gone as Momma.

"Follow her," says the Preacher.

The blond-haired guy and the huge man look back and forth at each other for a moment, but neither of them moves.

"But, Preacher," says the huge man, "she's going into them other woods. You know what they say about that place."

They're scared, I can tell. They've heard the same stories I have.

"*Follow her*," growls the Preacher, but he doesn't move either. I can see it all over his face. Even the Preacher is afraid to come after us. And he darn well should be.

Because we're going into the unknown parts of the forest, what I don't have any map for, all the parts where Gruff said never to go because there was people there, people who were worse than us, people who didn't even know the law we were fighting against. I'm dragging Tommy into the wildest woods, where the strange people are, men with splinters for teeth and women with three eyes, where all the ghosts walk around with skin on and wait to lay hands on you. Where haints wander, the spirits of bandits who never quit walking even after they died. I've heard so many stories. These are not the woods I know. These are not my safe places. Soon we're deep enough into the woods that I can't see the road anymore. We're coming close to lost.

EIGHT

keep the knife to Tommy's throat. He blubbers, he cries, but he doesn't fight me. It's like he knows this is his part.

"Please let me go," he says quietly.

"I can't. They'll kill me."

"I know," he says. "Will you let me go when we're safe?"

"Yes, Tommy. I won't keep you out in the woods with me forever."

But the second I say that my heart clenches up and I realize I don't want him to leave. I push the knife closer to his throat, as if to keep him from running away from me right now.

"You're hurting me," he says.

"Sorry," I say, and ease off a little. I push the knife into his back just hard enough for him to feel it but soft enough not to cut him. Just a little poke to keep some fear in him, to let him know that if he tries to run I got this waiting for him.

We walk until it's a fight to keep my legs moving. It's raining and I'm lost and I'm tired and I don't know how much farther I can go. Tommy's dragging. He kept stumbling into the knife so I don't hold it against him anymore, I don't want him to trip and hurt himself on it. For a while I keep the knife out, walking behind him, barking at him to pick up the pace. Then I just lead and he still follows me. He's as cold and wet and scared as I am. Sometimes I think I hear the Preacher or some of the Townie men behind us, but then it could be thunder, it could be a deer, it could be nothing at all.

Soon we hit a trail. This is a good sign, I just know it. Because Gruff told me something else about this forest too, a little fact I'm hoping the Preacher doesn't pick up on. Moon Haven lies just on the other side of these woods. At least, it does in all the stories Gruff told me. He said to take the long road around them, sure, that to cut through these woods was about the worst idea anybody could think of. But we don't have any other choice. Besides, I'd walk through just about anything to get back to Gruff. I just hope I listened right, that I got it all straight in my head. I hope I'm not leading me and Tommy into something even more horrible.

It rains hard now, the tree leaves dumping their water on us. I'm praying to Momma to save us, I'm praying for bread and not a stone, a fish and not a snake. My hair is wet in my face, Tommy's momma's dress is heavy and too big, sagging off me, leaving my shoulders naked to the cold. The hem is blackened by mud. My bare feet bleed.

Suddenly the path vanishes and I slip and fall face-first right at the mouth of a gorge, a deep one, dark and open like a gnarl-toothed smile. The knife goes sailing down and disappears. I begin to slip forward, my arms dangling into the black, my stomach sliding over the edge. I am going to fall. I'm going to fall and die forever.

Hands grasp my foot. I'm dragged backward, away from the hole, until my hands touch mud and wet leaves and I'm safe. I turn around and it's Tommy, still holding me by my foot. He sits down, shaking.

"I thought you were gonna die," he says.

We huddle close when we walk now. Tommy doesn't try to leave, even though I don't have a knife anymore. We walk until we see a hill, just a mound like a pimple sticking up from the earth, steep and sudden, and from the top of it smoke rises. Stuck in the middle of the hill is a door a little taller than me with a big metal bolt on it.

"We shouldn't go in here," I say. "We should keep going."

"Where to?" says Tommy. "We're lost. There might not be anywhere else."

He's shivering. I'm scared he'll get sick. Sometimes people would bring their sick kids to Momma and she would fix them with her magic. She was good at it, she could fix things way better than the doctor in town and everybody knew it. Sometimes, though, when they were shaking and shivering, there wasn't anything anyone could do but cry while they died. I don't ever want Tommy to die.

But then in the distance I see torches, hear the sounds of men in the forest. It's the Preacher. He braved the bad woods, same as I did, and now he's come for me. There's nowhere to run to. The lights are on all sides of us. My stomach tightens up and I can hear his voice in my ears, *Come to me, Goldeline, come to me,* until he's everywhere and all around me.

"What's wrong?" says Tommy.

"Don't you hear him?" I say. "Can't you see the torches?"

Tommy just stares at me like I'm going crazy. But I can hear the Preacher coming. I can feel him like a spider crawling across my neck. My eyes see spots and I'm breathing faster and faster and I'm scared, I'm so scared I might pass out, and then he'll find me for sure and I can't take it, I can't let him have me.

I run to the door and bang on it.

"Please," I call, "please let me in."

I bang the door harder, I hit it again and again. I beat the door with my fists and I kick and punch it and my fingers are bleeding and I scream and Momma please Momma please let me in.

The door swings open and I fall in on my face. Leaning not a foot over me is a short man, grizzled and crack-toothed, wearing a stained white shirt tucked into green trousers cut off at the knee. He's sitting on a little wooden cart with tiny wheels on the bottom. His pants end at the knee because that's where his legs end, and I can see the fleshy nubs like two elbows poking out at me.

"Well, look what the cat drug in."

Cats? Momma always said cats were good, a good sign is what she said they were.

"Get in if you're gettin'."

I stand up and shake my hair out like a dog. I look behind me to Tommy and he nods so we go in together. The man slams the door behind us. He scoots himself around by his hands, the wheels squeaking across the dirt floor. We're inside, and I don't know what world we just walked into.

The room is dark, lit by candles, a few wooden chairs, a chipped table with legs about a foot high with weird cuts in it like someone dragged a knife over the top. In the center is a broken clay pot full of browning flowers. No windows, just a lantern burning on the table and some stubs of white candles. Piles and piles of beets are stacked up on the floor, everywhere. A fire in the hearth flickers weird light over everything and a big black cauldron bubbles over the flames. It's like a happy home gone wrong, like what me and Momma had but twisted and sunk with grime. Whatever's cooking gives off an awful smell. I'd ask what stinks but it's not polite to ask what an awful smell is in a home if you're a guest in it. I might be an almost-bandit, but Momma taught me that much.

So I ask him where his kitty is.

"My what?" he says.

"You said you had a cat."

"Naw I did not." He spits in the dirt. "Filthy critters, cats. Mess everywhere. Worst-smelling mess there is. Worse than dog mess, worse than people mess. Hate cats."

The man wheels right up to me. Tommy's hiding behind me and I hold his hand tight.

"Let me get a look at you." His stubby fingers grab my jaw. He turns my cheek, brushes my hair out of my eyes. He smells real bad. "You're a pretty little thing. What's your name, girlie?"

"Goldeline."

"I'm Tommy," says Tommy.

"Did I ask you your name, little boy? Don't care about little boys. Little boys are varmints. Run around and muck up your garden. You a varmint, little boy?"

"No sir."

"Sir?" The man's laugh cackles out and falls into rasps. "No sirs around here. No sir. Nobody called me sir ever. You're a varmint, for sure, calling me a sir. Wish Momma could have heard that, a varmint calling me sir."

"I'm not any varmint," says Tommy. "I'm an orphan." He looks at me. "We both are."

"Don't go whining about it to me," says the man. "Everyone's an orphan if they live long enough. Done cried a lot when my own momma died. Death makes you hungry. Y'all hungry?"

I nod at him.

"Well, sit down then and I'll heap us up something."

The man scoots over to the counter and gathers three wooden bowls. He balances them on the cart and pulls himself over to the fire, to the cauldron where that awful smell comes from. With a big wooden spoon he ladles us full portions of soup. Tommy's nose is running and he's shivering all over. Hope he's too scared to show how bad it smells, lest he get us killed. I squeeze his hand and he squeezes back. It's good to know you're not the only scared one on the earth.

The man places the bowls on the table. Stink wafts up, like from a bog. We stare down at them.

"Sit down, will ya?" he says. I didn't realize we were still standing. Me and Tommy take our seats on the floor. "I'd sit down too, except I'm already sitting down. See, I ain't got any legs."

"I did see, sir," says Tommy.

The man wheels over to Tommy and sticks his grizzled beard up in Tommy's face. "What'd you say to me, little ginger? What'd you say to ol' Zeb?"

"Nothing," says Tommy.

"What's that, boy?" The man pulls a long carving knife off the table. "What you got to say to Mr. Zeb?"

"Mr. Zeb?" I say. "Is that your name?"

"How did you know that?" he says. He looks at me askance, eyes gone weird, like he's scared. "You a witch?"

I think about it for a second, but then I remember how much trouble witching got Momma into.

"No sir," I say. "That's just what you called yourself."

"I did?" he says. He points the knife at Tommy. "Did I?"

"Yes sir," says Tommy.

The man roars out a laugh. He's slapping the floor, cackling until he can't hardly breathe. He calms down after a minute, holding his belly like it hurts.

"Well, I guess I did then," he says. "Momma named me Zeb, rest her soul. Never knew my daddy. He run off when I was born. That's why I'm living in a durn hill, ain't it?"

He scoots over to a shelf from where he takes down a big jug. He guzzles from it till it's running down his beard. He wipes his face off and holds the bottle out to me.

"You want a drink, little girl?"

I sniff it and gag. It's worse than the soup.

"No thank you," I say, smiling as big and bright and sweet as I can.

"*No thank you*," says Zeb, mocking me, waving the knife in the air. "*No thank you, no thank you*. Well, at least miss prissy here's got some manners, don't she? What about you, little varmint? You want a drink?"

Tommy's face goes pale and sweaty.

"Uh-uh," he says. "Sir."

"Well durn," says Zeb. "Making ol' Zeb drink by himself. I guess that makes it about the same as every other night since my momma passed, don't it?"

He holds the bottle up high over his head in his right hand, like he's toasting a banquet hall full of people.

"To Momma," says Zeb, taking a long glug from the bottle. "May she rest in peace."

Zeb stabs the knife in the table, where it sticks like an exclamation point.

I think maybe Zeb was just messing with us, dangling that knife around. I think maybe Zeb is just a lonely old guy whose momma died, same as me and Tommy. I think maybe the whole world is a forest full of people like us, people who were born missing something, people who will never belong, people who wander the world lost looking for someone to share their lantern light with.

So why do the people in Templeton hate us so much?

A bang on the door.

"Two knocks in one night?" says Zeb. "Must be my lucky day." But he looks at me and sees how scared I am. "What's the matter with you?"

More knocks, and harder.

"Just don't tell him we're here," I say.

"Tell who?" he says.

"Please," I say.

"What kind of wicked you got on your tail, girl?" he says. "What did you bring to my house? Get back there behind the curtain and shut your mouth."

He points a crooked finger to the back of the room, where there hangs a tattered and patched red curtain. Behind it is a little washroom with a bucket and a cracked mirror. Also a hoe, a shovel, a wheelbarrow with a busted wheel, and an old rotting pile of beets.

"There's a hatch in there," whispers Zeb. "A hiding spot. Momma made it. When you get in, reach your arm out and pull that there sack over the hole. And don't you dare peep a word."

I shut the curtain while Tommy pulls the hatch open and climbs in. There's just enough room for me too. But I don't go down there yet. I want to watch him, the Preacher. I want to see. I peek through an eye-sized tear in the curtain.

Zeb opens the door. There stands a tall man in a long, rain-soaked black cloak, hooded like death or worse. Lightning glows the sky like angels behind him. I'm scared down to my fingers. He pulls back the hood. The wild white hair spills out all over the place. The candle light shines the scar down his cheek. It's the Preacher.

There's no door behind me, no way out of this washroom.

I keep both hands over my mouth so I don't even make a whimper.

"Pardon the intrusion. Raining like the dickens out there." He's dripping a puddle off his wet clothes right at Zeb's nubs. He shakes the rain from his hat and looks around the room. He stops at Zeb and makes a clicking sound with his mouth, like it's the first time he really noticed him down there. The Preacher kneels down to Zeb's eye level. "Hello, sir. It is a pleasure indeed to make the acquaintance of one of the Lord's unfortunates, especially on a devil-wrought night such as this."

Zeb hocks a big loogie. It slithers down the earth wall.

"What do you want?" he says.

The Preacher slits a grin, wide and shining.

"Little unfortunate, I will excuse your tone for ignorance. I'm acting interim deputy sheriff of Templeton. I am also a man of God and it would be good of you to address me as such."

"You mean you're a preacher. Never had much use for preachers," says Zeb. "Hollering up there, waving your hands around. Terrible way to spend a Sunday. Holy day you know, day of rest. Tired on a Sunday. Eat some stew and take a nap, that's about all I'm up to. Preachers never helped with the farm work. Preachers never did nothing for my old momma, heaven rest her bones."

Zeb scoots over to his bottle and drinks.

"State your business, Preacher. Dinner's getting cold."

"I'm chasing a fugitive girl," says the Preacher. "A tiny creature, white hair. Her mother was a dabbler in dark arts. A witch. She received her due punishment two years back, when I first began to reclaim this land for the Lord. The little girl has been working with some highwaymen. Notorious bunch, all degenerates and thieves. We got tipped off as to their location by a victim of theirs, a little boy who is also missing."

"Awful, such folk on this earth," says Zeb. He takes another sip of the bottle.

Tommy's hiding in the hatch, but he could get the Preacher's attention with just a sound. What if he gives me up? He could. It'd be his right. I kidnapped him, I did it with a knife. He could give me up right now and go home free. Tommy looks at me with his soft blue eyes and I know he knows it too. I hold up my finger to my lips, but I don't even have the knife to make him obey me. Right now Tommy can do whatever he wants. Right now my life is up to him.

"Fancy having a preacher in the house. I ain't seen another soul in months. Since Momma passed, it's just me here. I do good in the garden, digging up that ground. Love my garden. Spend all day out there. Growing stuff. Beets mostly. Love beets. You like beets?"

"I take delight in all of God's creation," says the Preacher. He smiles grandly, and it chills me full through.

Zeb scowls and spits again. "Beets are the hearts of the earth." He pulls one out of the pile, shines it on his shirt like an apple. He takes a big bite. "When you munch on a beet, that's what the earth tastes like."

"Do you live alone, little unfortunate?"

"Don't call me that. I ain't any unfortunate. Had my share of bad luck but I'm a man all the same. Made in God's image, same as you. I'm a sir."

"Indeed. Well, sir. Tell me now. Do you live in this decrepit mound of earth all by yourself?"

"I do. Ever since eighteen years back, when Momma died. Awful I tell you. Lonesome. I miss my momma. Hard to get around when you don't got legs. That's how I got into beets. Momma didn't like meat. Said, 'Every life is sacred.' Wouldn't hardly let us kill a cockroach. My dear old momma."

Zeb takes another glug from the bottle.

"And I take it you have not seen the fugitive girl and her captive little boy?"

"Ain't seen 'em. Night like this, probably fell in a gully."

Zeb lifts the jug up for another sip.

"Then why, sir, are there three bowls filled with that disgusting swill on your table?"

Zeb stops cold.

I should hide, but I have to watch. It's so hard to take my eye off the Preacher, like he commands it, like there's nowhere else in the world to look. I realize that's his magic.

That's how he gets folks to do what he wants. It starts with his voice, the rhythm and rise of his speech, like a melody that gets stuck in your brain, and before you know it you're singing along, believing every word. But it's more than just his voice. It's the whole way he is, his whole being. He's like a star falling. When the whole sky is full of burning things, the one falling is the only thing you see.

The Preacher lurches toward Zeb and grabs him by his collar. The jug goes clattering to the floor. He lifts Zeb high off his cart, until they are eye to eye.

"Have you seen the children?" he says.

"Yes," says Zeb.

"Are they here now?"

A silence. Just the rain, the thunder, the wind howling through the chimney. I pray to Momma to save me, I sing the nothingsong in my heart, I call down every ounce of spell or favor Momma ever might have had.

"Nope," says Zeb. "They long gone."

"Are you telling me they left without their supper? Back into the storm?"

"Didn't much care for beets," says Zeb. "Like you."

"If I pulled back that curtain, they wouldn't be there?"

"Nothing but my old wheelbarrow."

"Do you know that lying to me makes you an accomplice to murder? Do you know what accomplice means?"

"Means it's the same as I did it," says Zeb. "And ain't

nothing I've done you can pin on me, you preaching sack of dung."

"Are you certain these children are not here, sir?" roars the Preacher.

"Ain't no children here. I told you already, they left. Now leave me be and get your search on, lest they get farther away."

The Preacher drops Zeb on the ground, where he lies and moans. Then he turns and faces the curtain. The Preacher smiles.

He knows. I know he knows I'm here. I have to hide, but I can't move, it's like I'm transfixed, like the Preacher casts his own spell over me when he speaks.

"Awful lot of trouble for one little girl," says Zeb. "Don't you think?"

The Preacher fixes his hood back in place, like maybe he hadn't thought of that, like what Zeb said maybe bothered him a little. It's just a bit of a frown, like a dark bird that swooped across his face in a blink. It's enough for me to come back to my senses. I creep quiet and quick as I can to the hatch. Tommy's motioning me to hurry and I slide the sack over the opening just in time for the Preacher to rip back the curtain.

The silence is awful, just the rain and the Preacher's heaving breath.

After a few seconds Zeb speaks up from the floor.

"Told you there weren't nothing in there," he says.

"So you did," the Preacher says. "Good evening to you, sir." The door shuts and he's gone.

Zeb yanks away the sack and glares meanly at us.

"Bandits, eh? My, my, girlie, you are a right piece of bad, aren't you?"

"Thanks for saving us from the Preacher," I say.

"Shut up. I hate the law. Hate preachers too. Went to jail before. Me, in my condition. Doesn't matter to the law, doesn't matter to the preachers. The law's the law. And when the preachers are the law, well, it don't mean nothing good for folks like ol' Zeb." He spits a glob that hits Tommy's shoes. "Y'all just lay back here for the night. This ain't no inn. Earn your keep. Could always use some help around here. I'll put you to work in the morning."

He shuts the curtain and scoots off. I hear him bolt and chain the door at the mouth of the house. He's locked us in. There's no windows in here, no way out except the front door. We're trapped, at least until Zeb falls asleep. Maybe I can sneak the key from him then. I hear him talking to himself in the main room, clanking the jug down on his table. Me and Tommy crawl out of the hatch. The fire-glow under the curtain lights up our place: a pile of dirt, a wheelbarrow, a hoe. A pile of dead beets getting deader in the corner.

"Is the Preacher evil?" whispers Tommy.

"He's worse than you know."

"It's like when he's preaching he's saying words from the Book but they come out all wrong, like they've gone bad somehow. Spoiled. But I can't help but listen. I can't help but hear every word he says."

"That's about right, Tommy."

"I don't think Zeb is very nice either. I think we're in a bad spot."

"You think?"

His eyes well up again. I put my hand on his shoulder. "It's okay. The second he opens that door in the morning we got to run for it."

"You think that'll work?"

"I hope so."

"Shut up back there," hollers Zeb. "Can't a grown man talk to his momma in peace?"

"Look," I whisper, "let's just get some sleep."

It's dark even with the firelight. Dark like everything else, the whole world full of mean and wicked, even me, for letting all Gruff's men get caught. If it's true about me, that I'm wicked, is any of what the Preacher said about Momma true too? The thought latches on to my heart like a bat on a blossom.

"Thanks for not turning me in, Tommy."

He doesn't say anything. He just lies down next to me, and I put my arm around him, both of us a pitiful bundle of lonely and sad clutching each other in the dark. But it's okay, because I got a plan. I'll tell Tommy all about it tomorrow. Well, not all. See, I know where Gruff is. I know where I got to go.

Moon Haven. That's where he's heading. That's where me and Tommy got to go too. The Half-Moon Inn. Gruff's probably already there, waiting for me, a mug of ale, some roast duck, acrobats and magicians doing tricks all around him. Gruff is famous at the Half-Moon Inn, and when I get there I'll be famous too. They'll know all about me from the stories Gruff has been telling them. They'll know I'm the dreaded Ghost Girl of the Woods, me, Goldeline, that I'm the only little-girl bandit in the whole woods. They'll give me candy and dresses and dolls, but I won't take the dolls because I won't be just a kid anymore. They may think I am but they'll be wrong. When I get to Moon Haven, I'll be a bandit through and through. And if there's one thing Gruff taught me about bandits it's that a real bandit never gets caught.

First thing in the morning me and Tommy are busting out of here and taking off for Moon Haven.

NINE

"I'm sorry, little thing."

I blink my eyes open. It's real dark in the hill. Over me like a troll in a nightmare is Zeb. He's not in his cart, he's standing up a little bit, and he's got a red candle up to his face.

"I ain't evil," he says. "Not a bit."

"Zeb?" I say.

He sets the candle on the ground. In his other hand is a scrap of paper, symbols written on it, scribbled and gashed, no language I know.

"It's hard, just me out here, no momma to take care of me," he says. "Yes sir. Hard to tend a garden when you're all alone. Hard work keeping the rabbits out."

His face is so close to mine. I can see the dirt and food in his beard, and his breath smells like rotten things. Zeb bites his thumb until it bleeds. He smears a red streak across the paper, hooks it around like some strange letter, a symbol.

"Boy needs his momma around," he says. "Zeb needs a new momma. Hold still now, this won't hurt you none."

I try to jump up but Zeb grabs me. He's strong, stronger than I ever thought possible. I can't stand up. I scream loud as I can, I scream with everything I got held up inside me.

"Old magic," he says. "Word magic. This won't hurt none, but it will make you obedient." I gnash my teeth at him, I scream and spit. "Yes sir, you'll do everything I say. You'll be a right good helper for old Zeb."

He presses the paper on my forehead, and with his other hand takes the candle and tilts it down at me. Red wax drips from the candle onto my skin. It sizzles and burns, the paper now sealed to my forehead.

I feel it start, the color zapping out of my eyes, all sound going muffled and dull. I can't think anymore, my mind is clearing, it's so nice almost, to have no thoughts, to be free of Momma, of Gruff gone, of all my memories. There's nothing now, just a soothing blank as my thoughts blow away like smoke.

I'm going now . . . I'm going . . .

I got to fight it. I got to hold tight to Momma. I got to remember her.

Momma and me in our hut, laughing as the rain dribbles

down through a leak in the ceiling.

Momma singing paths through the woods, lighting the way with her song.

Momma mending baby bones with a word and a prayer.

Momma up on the scaffold, the Townies crowded round.

Momma jeered at, Momma mocked.

Momma's pain, the Preacher's torch glowing her face gold.

It all turns to hurt and I scream my hurt up into Zeb's grizzly awful face.

Suddenly the paper's gone, fluttered off somewhere. I don't know how but Zeb is lying on his side next to me, holding the back of his head. Maybe I did it. Maybe my scream was like magic.

But then I see flickers of Tommy in the candlelight, Zeb's hoe in his hand.

Zeb rises up to all fours. "You don't understand, boy," he says. "You don't know what it's like to work hard as old Zeb. You don't know what it's like to be out here, can't go a mile. You don't know what it's like to need and need and need and never get a thing. And I ain't ever gonna let you know. That kind of pain ain't for you. I'll fix you up good, ol' Zeb will."

Zeb scuttles toward Tommy, dragging himself through the dirt.

Tommy swings the hoe real hard this time. The hoe comes down on the back of Zeb's head. The candle snuffs out. I get up and pull open the curtain. Moonlight shines through a crack in the front door, lighting Zeb facedown in the dirt.

"Did I kill him?" says Tommy. His voice cracks.

I bend down over Zeb.

"Naw," I say. "He's still breathing. You knocked him out cold."

Tommy drops the hoe and sits on the floor next to Zeb.

"I conked a stranger in his own home," he says. "I'm on the run from the law. I'm a criminal now, aren't I?"

"But you're a good criminal, because you did it for me."

"Can somebody be a good criminal?"

"I think so. I hope so."

"I have to run now, don't I? I have to be on the run with you."

"No you don't," I tell him. "You can blame it all on me. I'll say I did it. You can leave now if you want."

He shakes his head. "I don't want to leave. I want to stick with you."

I smile at him, grateful despite myself.

"Let's look through this house and see what we can use," I say.

"You mean like stealing?" says Tommy.

"Of course," I say. "But good stealing. We're like bandits on the run, remember?"

"We're still the good guys, right?"

"Always, Tommy."

I step over to Zeb, soft and quiet as I can, and sneak the front door key out of his pocket. Zeb groans, but he doesn't get up. I know we have to hurry. I set about looking for things we can use.

Here's what I find: a rucksack with a strap on it. It's sturdy, made of leather. I needed a good pack. Inside I put three candles, Zeb's carving knife, a canteen that I'll fill with water from outside. In a trunk there's a bunch of old-lady clothes, and I take a gray hooded cloak for myself, like my old one, the one I left at camp. It's patchy and smells like feet, but it'll have to do.

Under Zeb's cot there's a tiny bag of coins, probably Zeb's whole life savings. I can fit it in my hand. It makes me sorry for him, a little, living alone out here, missing his momma. But then I remember him over me in the night and I shiver and I can't think about it anymore. I scratch the candle wax off my forehead.

"Could Zeb have done that?" Tommy says. "Made you obey him?"

"That was some bad magic Zeb was working," I say. "You should have felt it. It was like my brain was a flock of birds that up and flew off. It was like I couldn't think a thing if I wanted."

"I never seen real magic before," says Tommy. "I never even really believed in it."

"Well you best be believing," I say, ripping Zeb's paper

spells to shreds. "Seeing as we just found ourselves in a war-lock's den."

I put Zeb's momma's cloak on and turn to Tommy. "What do you think?"

"It stinks," he says.

"So does everything else in here. You ready to go?"

Tommy nods at me.

At the door I take one look back at Zeb slumped over on the floor. I wish he hadn't tried to magic me like that. Maybe we could have helped him, me and Tommy. Maybe we could have been his friends. But the way he talked about being treated by the Townies, by the law . . . well, why would he have expected us to treat him any different? I sing him a quick prayer and then shut the door behind me.

Outside the sun is just coming up, a gray dawn in the wet dripping world. We set out quick and quiet into the morning woods, like squirrels, like wood spirits, like the motherless bandit ghosts who will never get caught, who will never be killed, who will find their way to the big white inn in my dreams.

TEN

We walk without talking, watching the morning wake itself up and stretch out like a cat. Hummingbirds float around like asked questions and bash into each other over a purple flower. The woods are misty and hot with last night's rain, and the dew steams up from the ground like the forest's own breath. I should be scared, but I'm not. I'm walking through the new morning with my friend.

I don't quite know which way to go, lost as we are, but I know there's a road somewhere close maybe, a road worth looking for. We walk through thick woods and low tangled branches, around snake-dangling vines and spiderwebs taller and wider than me, down deer paths and lost ways. We pass foxes and raccoons and the slime trails of snails, the best kind who carry their houses on their backs, who are never lost, who can stop and always be home. But these woods aren't my woods. They're different, stranger, like there's a weird silver sparkle at the edge of everything, like any moment they could vanish and disappear and I'd be left in the gray fog of the world, nothing but God's big eye staring down at me. This whole forest gives me that feeling. I never felt anything like it before.

"You want to know where we're going?" I say.

"I didn't know we were going anywhere," says Tommy. "I thought we were just walking and hiding and being scared all the time."

"You think I'd lead you out here just to get lost?" I say. "Naw, Tommy, we're going someplace special. We're going to the best place in the whole Hinterlands."

"Where is that?" he says.

"We're going to Moon Haven!" I clap my hands together like it's the greatest thing anybody ever said, like he'll be so excited to know. But instead Tommy scowls at me.

"You mean the bandit town? I heard about that place. I heard it was rotten. They told us in church it was a den of sin and ini . . . iniquit . . ."

"Iniquity?"

"Yeah, that word. They said it was the most evil place in the world."

"So?"

"I don't want to go there," he says.

"Aw, come on. What they said about Moon Haven isn't true at all. You've seen the Preacher, what kind of liar he is. What makes you think the church folk are right about Moon Haven?"

"Well, my preacher is nothing like that guy. I never met any other preacher half as mean as the one who is after us. My preacher is nice and his name is Reverend Blackburn. Sometimes he lets me light the seven candles all by myself, and once he even showed me what all they make the incense out of. Reverend Blackburn said Moon Haven is a town of gambling and iniquity. He said it's just like the Two Tall Cities in the Book and that God's going to burn it flat down. I don't want to be there when that happens."

I want to tell him that the Two Tall Cities weren't burned up for being all wicked, but for not being generous to the poor, to folks like me and Momma. That's what gets a town burned up, not because there's some fun to be had there. Still, I don't think that would help much.

"Preachers just say that kind of junk because they're scared, Tommy. They're scared of all the good stuff in the world and they want you to be scared of it too."

"What's so good about a bandit town?" he says.

"First off, sure there are bandits in Moon Haven, but you and me are practically bandits now, too, so we should fit right in. Second, there's a place there, an inn, the Half-Moon Inn. It's the most wonderful place in all the world."

"What's so great about it?" he says, but I can tell he's interested. Now I just got to sell it to him good.

"Well, the food, for one. They got all kinds of food there. Funnel cakes and turkey legs and blueberry pie."

"They got cobbler?" says Tommy. "Blackberry cobbler's my favorite."

"Of course they have cobbler!" I say. "As much cobbler as you want. There's a grand ballroom in the Half-Moon Inn, and every night there's a different show. It's like a circus all the time. There's artists and musicians and magic. Good magic, Tommy, nothing like what Zeb tried to do. A theater too, with romance stories, and then the next night there's action plays, with sword fights and piano playing and dancing. It's a safe place in the world for weirdos, for the strange folk the world doesn't know what to do with."

"It sounds made-up to me," says Tommy.

"It ain't made-up. I swear."

"You seen it yourself?"

"Nope. But I heard stories. All kinds of stories. Not from any liar either. I promise on my heart." I lean in real close to him and whisper it in his ear, my eyes wide with the promise of it all. "Guess who isn't allowed in Moon Haven?"

"Who?"

"The Preacher," I say. "He can't even set foot in it. We'll be safe there, Tommy."

"The Half-Moon Inn have a post office?" says Tommy.

"So I can write to Aunt Barbara?"

My heart snaps a little bit with that. Tommy still has a person out there, still has some of his own blood. A family. That's okay, though. He'll need a place to go when I find Gruff. No way I'll be dragging Tommy along on me and Gruff's adventures. That'll be just us. It'll be good for Tommy to have a place to go after all this.

Tommy points over to a mess of trees and brush.

"You see that?" says Tommy.

He walks into the brush. The trees and vines are thick but Tommy pushes them back and away, following a little stone trail. And there it is, under a great big oak tree. A lone burned-black brick column, a chimney, stuck up like a bent finger from the grass. And right next to it is an upright piano. It's got vines wrapped around it, what looks like a bird's nest on top. Wildflowers bloom in purples and reds and golds surrounding it. The keys are brown and cracked, the wood all crawled on by bugs and spiders. It looks haunted.

Tommy walks right up to it, not scared a bit. "You think it works?"

"I wouldn't touch that if I were you," I say.

"Why? What could happen?"

A lot could happen, I think. I've read stories, I've heard Gruff and his boys talk around the campfire. These woods are full of bad magic. A bird could fly out. A spell could be broken. Trolls could come ambling from the forest. The piano might burst into flames. You might start playing and never be able to stop and have to play for forever until you're dead.

He reaches to press a key. I shut my eyes tight.

The note bounds eerily through the forest. It's quivery, not quite right, but rich and full as an old bird's call.

"It's a little out of tune," he says. "But it works."

Tommy begins to play. I never seen anything like it. His fingers dance across the keys, and the music that comes out is strong and fast and joyful, bellowing out like old Leebo used to do around the campfire. It's the bright sad music, my favorite kind, the whirling sort that picks your whole heart up like in a tornado and swirls it across the countryside.

Tommy strikes a key and half of it breaks right off into the grass.

"This one's busted," he says, and bites his lip. Then he does something wonderful. Slowly, humming to himself, Tommy plucks out a few notes that I know. It takes him a couple of tries, but then he gets it just right. The nothing-song, the one Momma taught me.

"How did you learn to play that?" I say.

"I dunno," says Tommy. "It's just that song you're always singing. You know, it's simple. Nice. I kind of like it."

"Play it again for me, please," I say.

He does. It's the loveliest way I've heard it since Momma died.

"Thanks, Tommy. I didn't know you could play."

He smiles at me.

"My daddy taught me," he says. "He was a good guy."

"I never knew my daddy," I say. "I don't even know what he looks like, or if he's alive or dead or anything at all."

"My daddy got sick and died. He was always getting sick, but he was a good guy. Me and Momma loved him."

"I thought you said he was a wrestler who fought river-boat captains."

"That's what I told all the kids in town. Really though he was a musician. He played piano. That's what he taught me, before he died."

I feel a little shiver of wind, a strange and cold breeze. It'll be getting dark soon. I'm already tired from all the walking.

"I don't think we should camp here," I say. "I think it's where a house burned down."

"How did the piano survive?" he says.

"I don't know, Tommy. But I don't think it's ours to find out."

He just nods at me, like he knows. We get to walking again, quiet this time, like we're trespassing, wandering through some dark stranger's woods and we don't want to get caught. The shadows from the trees feel cool, like this part of the woods is grayer, with less light, the spot of some sad mystery. The Preacher is out there somewhere, hunting us. We walk faster.

Soon me and Tommy come to a circle of trees. The circle was planted on purpose, like three hundred years ago somebody planted these trees for a reason, like it means something. But the feeling in them is good, like the people who planted them were good, like maybe we are part of the reason they planted them, somewhere in their hearts maybe they knew. An owl flies by overhead, big as the moon. The night is warm, and me and Tommy lie down together.

Soon he gets to dreaming, moaning softly in his sleep. I brush his hair, hush him, sing him a song. I wish Gruff were here. He always told me stories at night when I was afraid. Stories about things he'd seen in his travels, about a tattooed sailor whose skin knife blades couldn't cut, or strange maidens that lived in the woods and had one long tooth in their mouths to suck blood with. Or haints condemned to wander the forest, peeking into kids' windows at night, searching for the men who killed them. All Gruff's stories were scary, but they made me feel braver somehow, like if Gruff had faced these dangers and survived, then maybe I could too.

Soon I'll be back with him, when I make it to the Half-Moon Inn, when I've fought my way back to him. Just a few more days. Just a few more and we'll be back together again.

ELEVEN

When I wake up I'm so hungry I feel like my stomach's been empty for days. It hurts bad, like I spent all night getting kicked in the guts. Even with Gruff and his boys, I never went so long on just a handful of blackberries from the day before, same as I've never been so far from Templeton, so far from my own woods as I am right now.

Momma never had any reason to leave Templeton except for little errands she would run, journeys that didn't last more than a day or two. She never let me go with her, said they were secrets, not meant for little old me. Even as a tiny thing I had to fend for myself, but it was all right. I could make a fire, I had books. The animals would come to play with me. Momma would draw the star and the wolf into the dirt around our house, for protection. Nothing bad could happen to me if I stayed in the house. And nothing ever did. Not until I left it.

Momma never taught me to draw the symbols. I used to bug her about it when I was little.

"It isn't just the drawing," she said. "Anybody can draw a star in the dirt with a stick. It's what you put into it, what comes through you and into the stick. What makes the star gleam, what makes the wolf howl."

"Always just looks like stick drawings in the dirt to me," I said.

"That's because you don't see yet," said Momma. "It's the same with the songs. It's not the words, but how you sing them. That's why I taught you the nothingsong. It's the most powerful of all because there aren't any words. It's about whatever your heart makes it be about."

I didn't like not knowing anything. I figured I was old enough for the world. I wanted to talk to squirrels and have them talk back to me. I wanted the rabbits to show me where they hid their gold.

"Someday maybe you'll see, if you're all good and blessed and lucky."

"Then you'll teach me?" I said.

"I won't have to, Goldeline. By then you'll already know."

Momma was always saying stuff like that. Lot of good it does me now. For the first time maybe ever, I feel a little angry with my momma. Why is she not here now? Why didn't she teach me better? How are me and Tommy going to eat today?

Tommy sniffles. His head is in my lap. He's dreaming, making little dream noises, sighing. I poke him awake.

"We got to get moving," I say.

"What time is it?"

"Late," I say. "We have to go now, Tommy. It ain't safe to lie here and dream all morning."

Tommy looks out to the woods and shivers. We get to walking.

There's a strange wind out, hot and fire-smelling. I wonder if the Preacher hunts us in the day, or if he just walks his men through the woods with torches all night, calling out to us. The thought sends cold spiders up and down my back, and I walk us a little faster.

Above me and Tommy swoop birds. They touch on a branch and are gone, little brown ones. But no crows, no cardinals. I do see a blue jay, but I don't like them much. If you mess with their nests they'll go crazy on you. One time a blue jay nest fell out of a tree in front of our house. The momma bird went crazy, diving at us, trying to peck our eyes out. Gruff was there that day, visiting Momma. I didn't know him so well then. He was just Momma's friend.

"I'll shoot it if you want," he said.

Momma gave him a look that could have wilted an orchard.

"Sorry," he said.

It was strange being trapped in our own house, and kind of fun. Eventually Momma had to put on her heaviest cloak and run out to scoop the fallen nest up. She carried it out to the woods, the momma bird trying to peck her the whole time. After the nest was away from our house, the blue jay left us alone. A week later I went and found the nest. There were three dead baby birds in it. The momma bird had flown off by that point and left them. I dug a little grave and promised to bring flowers but I forgot until just right now.

I never brought flowers for Momma's grave either. I don't even know where she's buried. I know they wouldn't let her in a churchyard. But I don't like to think of Momma in a pit somewhere. I like to think of her as smoke, that she's in the air above us, sung out like a song.

That's how I like to think of it, sure. But if the Preacher catches me, will he burn me too? Will Gruff even know where to bring me flowers?

Me and Tommy walk for hours, till way after the sun has arced and headed on its way down to the dirt. Tommy's dragging. Both of us are tired, both of us hungry and thirsty. I got to think about hunting us some food somehow, catching some rabbits maybe. Something. I don't know how. It's not like we have time for me to stop and build a trap.

We come to the edge of a clearing and there's these two

cardinals on a branch together, just sitting there, red as fall leaves.

"Hello there," I whisper. "I been seeing a lot of you guys lately."

That's the sort of thing Momma used to say to birds, or really any kind of little creature. She'd face a squirrel on a branch and ask him what's what and he would tilt his head and chatter at her and she'd laugh and laugh. I'd ask her what the squirrel said and Momma would say, "Nothing for your ears, Goldy."

"But I want to know!" I'd say.

"Then listen," she'd say.

All I could ever hear were chirps and whistles, same as with the cardinals. It's pretty enough but it isn't words. It isn't stories. They tilt their necks and swivel their heads and fluff their feathers and mum up. It's like staring at pages of print before I could ever read a word. I used to just open a book and make up what was inside. Every book was about baby pigs who find a lucky mushroom.

"Why are you always talking to everything?" says Tommy. "If it's not a bird it's a bush or a flower. Like you got something wrong in your noggin."

"It's grown-folks stuff, not for kids. I'll tell you when you're older."

"Remember this kid right here saved your life two nights ago. This kid's only a year or two younger than you."

"Then it's girl stuff."

"Girl stuff is talking to birds?"

Why can't I ever understand things like my momma could? Maybe she was faking it. Making it up, like what I used to do with the books. That's a thought.

I look one of the cardinals dead in the eye and he winks at me. Then all of them take off into the air.

"That was weird," says Tommy.

"You think?"

"You're always such a . . ."

"Such a what?"

"Such a jerk! I mean it."

"Hush."

"I will not hush."

I clap my hand over his mouth. "You hear that?"

It was a voice, a rich, deep, chocolaty voice. A lady's voice, singing.

Tommy pulls my hand from his mouth. "Hear what? But wow, do you smell that?"

I do. It smells like hot cornbread. It smells like roast lamb and baked potatoes. It smells like the whole window of a pie shop. It smells like a rich kid's house on Christmas, the smell that would waft through the windows and catch me like a trap and send me home hungry every holiday in Templeton. It smells like a whole world of delicious, and it's coming from the clearing right up ahead of us.

"Careful," I say. "Could be anybody out there waiting for us."

"I don't care who they are," says Tommy, "so long as they got cornbread."

He runs off through the trees, and I follow him hollering.

We hit the clearing and the sun blasts us so strong I have to squint my eyes. The field erupts with purple and yellow wildflowers, bright as candy. It stretches almost two hundred feet all around and is stuffed with the sweetest smells, honeysuckle and better. Butterflies blink and twitter around me like happy thoughts. The grass under my feet is the softest I've ever felt. Everything in this place is alive. The flowers seem to turn their heads and stare at us.

"Tommy?"

He's laughing, running toward the smell. But when he sees where it comes from he stops.

At the edge of the clearing, right before it fades into forest again, is a house. A big blue thing sat eight feet up in a tree that comes down through the floor like a big fat chicken leg. It doesn't look like a tree house though. It looks like a real house, with a roof and a chimney. It's like somebody took a house off a street somewhere and stuck it in this tree. I've never seen anything like it. The house leans down toward us like it's trying to hear what we're saying. It's got one big window facing us like a great eyeball, but the curtains are drawn and I can't see inside.

"I'm scared," I say.

"But it smells so good," says Tommy. "And I'm so hungry."

I feel the tug in me, the tiny invisible string attached to my insides, pulling me forward. The sweet singing louder and louder in my ears.

"I know that song," I say.

"What song?" says Tommy.

"It's a song Momma used to sing me. It's her cooking song."

"Goldeline," says Tommy, "there isn't any song."

"Of course there is. It's all over the place," I say, pointing to my head. "It's right here in my ears."

"Y'all just gonna stand there yapping or you gonna come up to my house?" The voice is a lady's voice, thick and rich as gravy, like a fat grandma voice. It sounds old and warm as a family quilt.

Me and Tommy look at each other.

"Y'all late," says the voice. "Dinner's been ready for a long while now. Y'all coming up or not?"

"Excuse me, ma'am," says Tommy. "But we don't know how to get up there. To your house."

"Try the ladder," says the voice.

A rope ladder hangs down from an open trapdoor in the house's floor. I don't know how we both missed it before.

"Bunch of hungry kids I cooked for," says the voice. "Now come on up the ladder and let me feed y'all. 'Cause I know y'all are hungry. I been knowing that for about two weeks now. I got plans. Now come on up and stop making me wait on my own dinner."

"I think we should go," says Tommy. "Don't you?"

My first thought is *Of course we shouldn't. Don't you know what happens to hungry kids who go into strange houses?*

But the singing is so loud, so sweet. It's right inside my ears, I can almost taste it. It reminds me so much of Momma, like she's right here with me, something that isn't just me remembering. I feel the tug of the invisible string, the desire to go. I want to go up to her house. I have to.

"Please?" says Tommy.

"I don't know."

"Please, Goldeline? Please?"

I know her song, Momma's cooking song. The song means it can't be bad. The song means it has to be a good thing. Besides, I'm so hungry.

"Let's eat," I say.

"Are you sure?" says Tommy.

"Of course," I lie.

I test the rope ladder with my foot and it's sturdy. I haul myself up and through the floor into the tree house.

The house is crammed full of furniture, clothes, knick-knacks. I've never seen so much stuff piled up anywhere, not to mention in one single house. There's a giant wood table with heaping plates full of cornbread and roast duck and turnip greens and mashed potatoes and beans and rice and gravy for days. The table has three chairs around it, just for us, carved with symbols of owls and stars and wolves. A blue fur hangs on the wall next to a carving of an old man holding a skull. There's a woodstove and a kettle fire and shelves and shelves of books, more books than I've ever seen in my life, thick books and skinny books and books with pages hanging out of the bindings. A giant spoon and fork are nailed to the walls like they were paintings, jars full of roots and vegetables and spices hang from the ceiling, a wall of plates and pans and pots and a row of cooking knives hanging like icicles, an opossum mounted with its fangs poking out. A massive clock shaped like a church tower leans a little toward us as if it could topple over and smash everything at any minute. It's just the kind of home I've always wanted, wild and full of wonders.

Moving all through the chaos is the fattest lady I've ever seen in my life. She's in a red dress down to the floor and she seems to glide like a giant floating strawberry. She has big red cheeks and the biggest belly and she's singing that song. It's my momma's song and it's my song and it comes straight from her heart, she doesn't even have to sing it. Her blue eyes sparkle, her gray hair is all bunned up on her head, her hands are big and wide and in pretty white gloves. I want her to hold me. I want to lay my head on her chest and sleep for days.

Already I love her. I don't know how, but I do. I feel like I've known her my whole life and longer.

"Are you my grandma?" I ask, and I don't even mean to.

"No, child. I'm nobody's grandma. But you can call me Bobba."

"Bobba's kind of a grandma name," says Tommy.

I'm so enchanted by the house I didn't even hear him come up behind me. It's the most beautiful house I've ever seen. There's a stuffed raccoon hanging off the wall and when I touch its fur it bristles.

Bobba smiles at Tommy. She's still got all her teeth.

"Now sit on down," she says. "Calling me grandma. Lay all y'all's stuff down, now, we are fixing to eat. Set your heavy bag down, right there, right by your chair."

It seems like a miracle, but there's an empty spot in the house, just big enough for my pack. I feel my shoulder ache from it, where it's worn me down red and raw. I lay the pack down, with everything me and Tommy got in the world in it, Zeb's money, his momma's cloak. I set it right down and all of a sudden feel lighter, freer, the whole weight of what we've done and what's been done to us and where we have to go next and the Preacher and Gruff and Momma, all of it gone, even if it's just for a moment.

"Don't that feel good?" says Bobba. "Don't it feel good to lay your troubles down?"

It does. It feels wonderful, like coming home. I feel freer

than I've felt since Momma died, since before I took off to the woods with Gruff. I haven't felt so good in ages.

"You two look like the Evil One crawled up and bit you. Seen winter rabbits look less starved than y'all two. Sad days, children running around, needing old Bobba to cook for them just so they don't starve to death. Heaven almighty, bad times afoot, good Lord."

"We are pretty hungry," says Tommy.

"Then eat, sweetheart. Been cooking all day for y'all."

"How did you know we were coming?" I say.

"Oh, old Bobba has her ways. Shush up and eat now. We'll talk about all that later."

"Are you magic?" says Tommy.

Bobba smiles a little smile and holds a fat gloved finger to her lips.

It's okay. I already knew she was anyhow. Something weird in my blood that's been there since always, something that was Momma's—that's what told me. That's how I knew Bobba was magic.

We eat. The food never seems to run out, and it's been so long since we've had a real meal. I eat and eat and somehow I'm not even full yet, not close, not even after four helpings of mashed potatoes and gravy, which is my favorite. I eat until my plates are stacked and my stomach is so filled up the food just sits in my mouth, I can barely even swallow it. I've never been so full in my whole life. I'm so full it hurts.

But then I get a whiff of the hot blackberry cobbler as Bobba pulls it fresh and steaming out of the oven and I gasp out loud.

Bobba laughs.

"Best blackberry cobbler this side of the river, you can bet on it." She claps her hands. "But dessert comes in its own time. Now it's time for tea."

Bobba pours out two cups of tea and they sit steaming in front of us. She dabs honey and a big block of sugar and a little milk in each.

"I never had tea before," I say.

"I have," says Tommy. "I don't like it. Can we skip the tea and just go ahead and have dessert?"

"Why you think you can skip tea? Civilized folk always have tea right at four o'clock, and it's four o'clock now. I learned that in the Northlands. Y'all ever been to the North-lands?"

"I never been anywhere," says Tommy.

"Figured as much. Y'all two wandering around here, whole world on y'all's backs, never even been out past the river. Hard to believe that's what it comes to, two stupid kids or the whole Hinterlands is lost." Bobba does her laugh again, her whole big warm body shaking with all the happy. It makes me laugh, Tommy too. We laugh ourselves about silly.

"Can I eat cobbler now?" says Tommy.

"Not until every drop of your tea is drained," says Bobba.

"But I don't want any tea!" says Tommy. "I want pie! I want cobbler! I want it all now!"

I take a sip of tea. It's scalding hot and weirdly bitter, like chewing on something straight out of the ground. I feel it slide down my throat and slither into my stomach and my stomach turns a little. I don't like tea I don't think. Still, I want the cobbler. I want the pie. I've never wanted anything so bad in my life.

Bobba slices out a huge slab of cobbler and places it daintily on a plate in front of me. "Finish your tea and it's all yours," she says.

I have another sip, then a gulp. It's cooler now. My mouth feels tingly, like when you lick an icicle.

"Gimme some cobbler too!" says Tommy.

"Fine, fine," says Bobba. "No need to be fighting over Bobba's cobbler now. Famous cobbler. Best cobbler in the land." She heaps a steaming purple glob onto his plate. But her smile cracks a little bit, just at the edges. I can see it now, the yellow of her teeth, the little fractures in them like veins, all the powder on her face, the pinch marks on her cheeks, the great false red of her lips. It's all a story, and I can read it maybe, I can read it if I try hard enough, if I wasn't so full, if my mouth wasn't so numb, if I hadn't drank so much tea.

Tommy sniffs the tea. "Gross," he says. He pinches his nose.

"Sip, don't gulp," says Bobba, with a full wide wolf grin now. "Little heathens. Gentlemen don't gulp."

Tommy downs the whole cup in one big slurp.

"Oh boy!" he says, clapping his hands together.

We both eat and eat, and then have seconds, and then eat more. My stomach hurts from all the cobbler, from the sweet, from the mashed potatoes, from my whole last few days in the forest.

"Y'all going to eat it all, ain't ya? Not leave a bit for Bobba. Don't anybody ever leave anything for Bobba." She leans her head down against her gloved palm, elbow on the table, and looks out over all the dishes we cleaned, the empty pans, the dirty napkins strewn all about, me and Tommy eating everything up as fast as we can. "Now how did y'all go and work up an appetite like that?"

"We're getting chased," says Tommy, mouth full of dessert.

I kick him under the table.

"Gracious Lord!" says Bobba. "Now who in the world would want to be chasing y'all two?"

"The Preacher," says Tommy. "I didn't think he was evil at first but now I'm pretty sure he is. See, he wants to kill us."

I kick him harder.

"Ow," says Tommy. "Stop kicking me."

"Then shut your mouth," I say, then look toward Bobba. "My momma always told me that kids should keep quiet at dinner. They should eat their dinner and be quiet and keep grateful."

I see a flash of something in Bobba's eyes. I put my fork down and study her a minute. She's way too big to be climbing up any rope ladder. The house would have to kneel down like a good horse to let her up in it. If she ever leaves at all. Oh, she's got to leave. How else could she get all this food up here? Still, something doesn't figure right. Bobba keeps making these little stitching motions with her fingers, like she's unspooling thread.

"A preacher! My, my," says Bobba. "Hate preachers. Awful men, the worst there is. Good enough intentions, sure, but it takes a certain kind of fool to think he can speak for the Lord. A servant's heart, they say. Vain heart's more like it. Preacher's the vainest type of man. Loves power, respect, even money. Certainly money. Because there's a fortune to be made off of God, no two ways about it. Preachers have the keys to heaven. They can bind and loose, lock and unlock. Awful lot of power preachers have."

"Yeah, this guy is nuts. I seen him. I rode in a carriage with him," says Tommy. "Can I have some more cobbler?"

"Sure, baby," says Bobba. She slops a steaming, gurgling mess of blackberry cobbler down in front of him. Stuffed as I am, my stomach scoots itself over and makes some room. I can almost taste the sweet goodness in my mouth. "See, I know this preacher y'all talking about. He wasn't so bad when he was young. Course, he got corrupted, spent his years in the desert. Desert my tail. Just wandering around, whipping on himself, talking to those fanatics up north, wanting to set folks on fire. Five years he was gone, had to be, off getting his head filled with all kinds of garbage. When he came back, well, he wasn't the same old preacher, and that's the truth."

Bobba knows the Preacher? We shouldn't be here. Why are we still here? Why am I still hungry? Why haven't I grabbed Tommy and bolted out of here already? Her fingers twitching, pulling invisible thread. Is Bobba doing this?

"Tommy was just teasing," I say. "Nobody's chasing us. Just a game we've been playing. We got lost. We were traveling with my uncle, Uncle Gruff. We just got to meet back up with him on the road, that's all. Then everything will be right as rain."

"Nope," says Tommy. "Nothing will ever be right again."

The room goes full quiet, except for the ticking of the great big clock and the clink of silverware against the plates.

"Tommy?" I say.

"Go ahead," says Bobba. "Tell me all about it."

Bobba's fingers are moving fast, unspooling and unspooling, like she's pulling the answer from him, like she's unwinding the truth.

"We're going to Moon Haven because that's where Goldeline says we'll be safe. But we're criminals now. I don't think we'll ever be safe again."

"That's enough, Tommy!" I jump up to my feet and grab his hand. "Thanks, Miss Bobba, but we got to go now."

"Sit down!" she thunders. The candles flicker and darken, the whole house shakes.

Tommy's face falls into his cobbler. He doesn't get up.

"You don't remember me, do you, child?" says Bobba. "You don't remember anything. Your momma did that, put a wall up in you. She didn't want you to have to remember anything nasty, anything unpleasant. Yep, your momma just whisked those memories right out your pretty little skull."

I try to run, but I can't. Invisible arms push me back down to the chair. I can feel their warm fat fingers on my skin.

"Let me go, please. I won't tell anybody you're here. We'll just disappear off into the woods and be gone, like you never even saw us."

My vision swirls and I feel so hazy. I try to stand up, to reach over to Tommy, but I can hardly move. I feel like I'm in a tub of warm water, a bath full of flowers, the scent so strong it turns my stomach and makes me float.

"Is Tommy dead?" I say.

"No, honey, but he might wish he was, before all this plays out," Bobba says. "Y'all two got one ghastly journey to take before it's all over."

"Did you poison the tea?"

"The tea? Naw. I poisoned the air," she says. "And y'all

been breathing that air ever since you first stepped into Bobba's field."

"Why are you doing this to me?"

"Because, sweets," Bobba says, reaching up to the great bun of gray hair on top of her head. She lifts it, showing me a bald veiny egg of a skull. Long scars streak across her head, like claw marks, or maybe even burns. Did the Preacher do that to her? Is Bobba another woman he burned? She places the wig on the table and clears her throat. She slides off her gloves. Her hands are massive, hairy, with fingernails long as wolf fangs. "It's like the Book says, if you bring forth what is within you, it'll save you. But if you don't bring forth what is within you, well, that'll destroy you. Do you understand?"

I try to run but I can't, I can't even move, my stomach hurts, my head throbs, all the colors blur and smear together like a meadow of flowers. Bobba grabs my head and pulls my face to hers. I can see the green-gold swirls in her eyes, smell the dead-meat rank of her breath. Her hands are cold on my cheeks and her nails dig into my scalp.

"I need you to remember," she says. "For your sake, and for your momma's."

Eyes wide open, pupils spiraling into mine, Bobba kisses me straight on the lips. My sight goes black, and I'm gone.

TWELVE

'm in a meadow. There's a tree at the end, the same tree that Bobba's house sits on, but there isn't any Bobba's house on it. In a knot in the middle of the trunk somebody wedged a book. I pull it out. It's warm and throbbing and soft. When I open the book it makes a cry like a baby and I shut it real fast. In the limbs of the tree are about a hundred cardinals, so many I think they're leaves at first. They chirp and flutter and all at once rise, the flock of fire flies off past the sun and I fly off too, so high the trees look tiny, the whole world the size of a gumdrop, my face pressed against the sky like it was a mirror, the cold glass on my cheek looking at my face, but it's not my face, not quite.

It's not me at all. It's my momma. I'm looking at my momma.

This is a memory.

One that is too old for me to remember, a forgotten one like a scar on my head that hair grew over and covered.

It's Momma, young and white-haired and beautiful. Momma I love you. Momma how I missed you. She smells sweet as fresh rain, like honeysuckle. It's the smell that hurts so bad. She picks me up and spins me and it's like I'm float-ing upward, like a raindrop in reverse. She kisses me and I'm so small, I'm a baby. I know this is true because it feels true, but how could I remember being so small? Her face against mine is the softest thing I ever felt.

Bobba is there too, but she's sweeter, gentler. Her hair is real and silver and wild all over her head. She has cobbler with her but I can smell all the good in it, it wasn't made mean and wicked like what she made me and Tommy. She hugs Momma like a sister and they are close, they laugh together.

I'm in Momma's house, with the thatched roof and the stove and the rocks, the ones with the little birds on them, the ones Momma taught me with. The books in the corner stacked and good-smelling, I don't know how she got them but there were always more whenever I wanted. The lantern I used to carry when I wandered the woods at night. But I was never scared, even in the dark nighttime, because of the songs Momma taught me, the nothingsong that sparkled the air when I sang it, that protected me from all the scary stuff in the dark, the horror of night like it says in the Book, the fanged things, the wolves and snakes and wicked men, my little light out in the black woods. I would wander and sing and pretend I was a star that fell out of its tree and toppled to earth but didn't burn out, just got small and brave and became a girl who glowed at night. It was impossible to be scared when you could glow.

The light scares the mess out of the darkness, you can believe that.

There's a flicker in my eyes and I'm in Bobba's tree house again, but it looks different, all ragged curtains and brown, gunk-filled plates and rats gnawing bird bones off the floor. Bobba's hideous scowl is a foot from my face, her eyes red and ripped-looking. She slaps me.

"No!" she says. "You got to remember!"

Bobba slaps me harder and my lip busts, and I can feel the blood go hot on my chin. It's the blood that does it, and I'm back in the forest, back wandering, and it's cold but not horrible cold, just enough that everything has a snap to it. It's another memory. I'm a kid again, maybe five or maybe four, and I have my cloak and my lantern and I'm singing the nothingsong but it comes out all wrong because I'm sick and my throat hurts, I croak and caw the song like a bullfrogbird, like something with leather wings that lives in the mud.

I feel sick and I feel lonely and I hate my momma for making me wander out so late, so tired. I was already mostly asleep when Momma shook me awake and said, "Put on your cloak, Goldeline, take your lantern!" and I said I didn't want to but she said it again, "Baby darling, please, you got to, Momma needs you to. Quick! Up to it! Go now! Shoo! Shoo!" and I've been wandering and wandering since. Hours maybe. The rule is, when something secret happens, Momma sends me out to the woods and I can't come back, not until she lights a candle in the window to guide me back with. That's the rule, and never ever have I broken it. But tonight I'm sick and the night is full of crows, the clouds running fast as rabbits across the sky. A storm is coming. There's the burned-leaf smell in the air, the stench of a bad one way far off. The trees bend and stretch. An owl looks at me with big strange eyes. I think it's blind. Nothing in the world feels right tonight.

Even though I'm not supposed to, even though I never broke a promise to my momma before, I start my walk back to our house early, even though Momma hasn't lit the candle. See, I know the way, these woods are my own and I can't ever get lost in them, not anymore, not so close to our little house. I sneak right up to the window and take a peek in.

Inside is a man. He's got his back to me. Momma's smiling at him, this sad kind of smile I've never seen on her face before, like I never seen her look at anyone in my whole life. Neither of them see me. I don't understand what's happening, all I know is that it's something bad.

But the wind blows and the moon dims out and it all fades. I can hear Bobba screaming at me, screaming somewhere long and far off, *No! No! You got to keep going! You have to see!* But I'm tired, and there's a bed for me, I can feel it, my old soft bed, Momma's there too, with my quilt, and it's warm, warm, and I can't stop myself now, and soon I know I'll be asleep and dreaming again. I hope I hope I hope for good dreams.

THIRTEEN

wake up slumped in a hard wooden chair. Tommy's still face-down in his plate, but instead of cobbler now it's just a pile of old chicken bones. I'm scared he's dead but then I realize he's snoring. I've never been so happy to hear snoring before in my whole life. We're in a room, a small one, dusty and ruined. The table is a dead gray color, like old skin, chipped and dented. Torn shreds of paper and the covers of books cover the floor. A rank nutria hide is nailed to the wall. A rat scampers over my feet. No Bobba in sight. I try to stand but have to sit right back down again. I'm woozy and confused. Sunlight spears through a chink in the roof, and bats hang like rotten teeth from the rafters. Where am I? I pray a little to Momma.

Momma my head hurts. Momma is this Bobba's house?

The gnawed bones on my plate, crusts of moldy bread on the floor. Is this what we ate yesterday? But it had tasted so good. It tasted as good and lovely as the house looked, like a real home for me. Was it a trick, a dream? Or was it Bobba's poison?

Tommy's still snoring away on the table. Ants crawl a little speckled line over his hand, medium-sized ants like watermelon seeds. I brush them off and poke him awake.

"Hey, Tommy."

He moans a little and blinks at me. A sun shaft hits him bright on the face and makes him glow a little like a saint in a picture book.

"Are we dead?" he says.

"Nope," I say.

"My stomach hurts."

"Yep."

"My head hurts too."

"Uh-huh."

"I didn't get to finish dessert."

"Better be glad about that."

Tommy sits awake. He looks scared.

"Where is she?"

I shrug.

"This is the same house, right?" he says.

"I'm not sure."

"But it's got to be. It's the same size and everything." He

sniffs the air and coughs. "Why is it so horrible now?"

"I don't know, Tommy," I say. "It's like Bobba could control it. What it looked like to us, how it felt. Like she was giving us whatever we wanted."

"She was all in my dreams," he says. "She was huge, like a big old walrus. She kept saying, 'Eat a biscuit! Put some jelly on it! Get a little sugar in your blood!'" He shakes his head. "I don't feel too good."

"Let's get on out of here, Tommy. The rope ladder still works, I think."

I try it out. The rope is scraggled and rough and it cuts my hands, but I make it down okay. Tommy takes a step and falls smack down in the tall grass. He stands up, then topples over and vomits. I let him finish, and then I pat him on the back.

"Was that magic?" Tommy says, wiping drool from his chin. "Last night I mean?"

"Yes, Tommy," I say. "You believe yet?"

Even the field looks different today. Spiderwebs, maybe a hundred of them, stretch from grass blade to grass blade, and the dew makes little jewels across the thread. Bobba's house hangs sad on the tree, drooping like a bowed old-lady head. There isn't any book in the tree either, not like in my dream. How can this be the same place as yesterday? Other than the spider diamonds, there's nothing magic about this meadow. It's just weeds and ugly. Not even any real flowers, only anthills and a weird dead-skunk smell.

I don't know what to make of my dream. No, it wasn't a dream. It was a memory, real as I just lived it. I was remembering something fierce, something lovely and awful. I know it was important.

Then I remember Momma, her cheek against mine, being safe, a baby in her arms. I drop my hair over my face so Tommy can't see me cry.

"I'm thirsty," he says.

"Hold up a minute and let me get you some water."

I'm glad to get away. My pack's lying over in the grass, the canteen spilled out next to it. Guess Bobba chucked it out the tree house when she left. The stopper's off. I pick it up and shake it. Empty. We don't have any food either. I feel awful all over. But all of Zeb's money is still there, so at least Bobba didn't rob us.

"Old ugly warthog," I say, and wince as a pain flashes through my skull. She tricked me, yep, maybe even poisoned me. But she gave me something too, something important. I just got to figure out what it means.

I got to get to Moon Haven, to Gruff. He'll know what to do. If I can get to Gruff then everything will be okay. He knew Momma, he was around her even when I wasn't. Maybe he knows who the man in my memory was. Maybe Gruff will know what to do.

"I'm hungry," says Tommy.

"I guess I would be too if I just yucked up my whole dinner."

"Thirsty too."

"Then get up," I say, "and let's get to walking. No food here, unless you want to kill and cook a crow."

"Not on your life," he says. He looks woozy and I think he might puke again.

I don't know why, but in this moment I've never been more grateful for Tommy. I run over and give him a hug. He smells awful and I kind of regret it but also I kind of don't, not at all.

"What was that for?" he says.

"You looked like you needed it."

"What does that mean?"

"Hush up and walk, it means," I say.

Tommy follows me out of the clearing and back into the dark creeping woods.

We've been walking a few hours, and we're pretty bad lost. Tommy keeps throwing rocks in the woods, following behind me, humming to himself. I found us some berries, but they were sour, and we haven't come to any water anywhere. I keep saying I know where we are and I know where we're going, and Tommy keeps acting like he believes me.

But the nice thing about being lost is that, you wander far enough, you always wind up somewhere. That's what Gruff used to say. *If you're lost, Goldy darlin', all you gotta do is keep going. So long as you're moving, you ain't lost. You're getting somewhere.* I can already see the Half-Moon Inn, where Gruff will be waiting, a plate of hot chicken and mashed potatoes in front of him, a mug of ale in his hand, a fat cigar clenched in his teeth, laughing about how couldn't anybody catch him, not some sucker Preacher anyhow. You couldn't catch him because he was a ghost, how women trembled and men turned up their collars when they passed through our woods. That's how he used to brag when he was good and laughing by the fire. That's how he'd brag when he picked me up and spun me and held me close to him and we were like a family. Or at least the closest thing I've come to a family since my momma died.

But you can't replace a momma. Nothing can ever fix that. It's the kind of cut that throbs in your sleep, gets hurting with the wind and with a memory, that splits open all the time and spills blood all over the place just when you think you finally got it healed. That's what I know about losing a momma. And I'm starting to understand that maybe I'm going to have to keep knowing it for the rest of my life.

"Whatcha thinking about, Goldeline?"

"Not a thing, Tommy. Just water and some food and some somewhere else."

"Are we lost?"

"Sure are."

"Oh," he says. "Well, I'm glad I'm lost with you."

But then me and Tommy come up on something I don't expect at all. The forest ends suddenly, and ripped through and clear is a road, bread-colored, six feet wide and dusty. A good one, I can tell from the wheel tracks. One that's in use a lot.

"This is it, Tommy! This is the road to Moon Haven. It has to be."

"What makes you so sure?"

"I don't know," I say. "I can just feel it. I know this is the way."

"I don't know, Goldeline."

"What's not to know?"

"Well, it just don't feel good," says Tommy. "In my stomach I mean."

"Probably still sick from Bobba's food."

"Not that kind of not feeling good," he says. "I mean in a big way. Like something bad's waiting on us."

"What could be bad at Moon Haven? This is where we've been headed. It's where we'll be safe."

"People haven't been real friendly to us, Goldeline. Everyone we meet wants to kill us or poison us or make us sick. What makes you think this place will be any different?"

Because Gruff will be there, you idiot. But I don't dare say that.

"I'll tell you what Moon Haven means," I say. "Moon

Haven means food. All kinds of food, and good stuff, not poison or magic or anything. Real food. It means a bed for the night, a comfy one, with as many blankets and pillows as we want. We got money, right? What we took from Zeb. And there's no way they've heard of us all the way out here. Because we're a long way from Templeton, a long way from where the Preacher would be headed."

But right as I say that, something flinches in my belly. Just a whisper of something, like a ghost wind saying maybe we're not near quit of him. That maybe he's going to follow us for always.

I can't tell Tommy that I feel the Preacher's eyes on me, even now. That I mean something to him, something important. I can't say what, or why either. But I matter in all of this. It has something to do with my dream, with my memory. I matter so much he won't stop until I name him or he kills me.

Name him? Those aren't even my words. Those are somebody else's. Those snuck into my brain from the wind, from the red-burned sun, from the clouds reflecting in the puddles along the road. Something is pulling him to me, dragging him along, and it won't be finished till one or the other of us is dead.

"You all right?" says Tommy. "You look like something got you spooked."

"We'll follow the road to Moon Haven, like I said. We'll

be safe in Moon Haven. And there will be acrobats at the Half-Moon Inn. It'll be like a carnival, lanterns strung up, torches, musicians on every corner." I tell all Gruff's stories again, say them out loud like they're some kind of magic spell, like the harder I believe them the more they will protect me. "So much food you can't even imagine it, a banquet hall with a table so long you got to squint to see the people on the other end of it. Everything we could ever want or need is in Moon Haven, I guarantee you."

"Acrobats?" he says.

"Yep. Dancers too."

"Musicians?"

"You bet. Street singers all over the place. I bet we can even find you a good piano to play on."

"Yeah, I dunno." But he's smiling. He's even got a whistle to him. "It'll be something, won't it?" He flicks an acorn off into the leaves.

I'm so happy I could run the whole way there. By nightfall I'll be with Gruff and we can run away together, be bandits on the run from the preachers and the lawmen and the Townies forever and ever, never belonging anywhere, with no one and nothing to ever drag us down. Safe, me and my Gruff, together finally at Moon Haven.

FOURTEEN

We creep alongside the road, deep into the trees where no one but another bandit could see us. We keep the road just in sight, just visible, so we don't lose it. Twice carriages pass us, twice me and Tommy duck down in the weeds, and twice they move along. A few men on horseback ride by, their collars up and hats down even in the heat, as if they know bandits are afoot. I wonder if it's me and Gruff that's struck the fear in them or something else. My belly's gnawing itself like it's got teeth. We still got Zeb's money. Maybe I'll buy us something sweet. Maybe I'll buy us a pie.

We come to a road sign, a chunk of wood with some words carved into it, the only words I ever want to see again for the rest of my life. "Moon Haven ½ Mile." I can't believe it. Moon Haven was just past the bad woods, same as Gruff said it would be. I'm so happy my guts hurt, my heart gallops in my chest.

"That's where we're headed, right?" says Tommy.

"That's it," I say. "We're almost home free."

"Good," he says. "I'm awful tired of walking."

"Not too much farther at all."

I start to sing a different song, a happy one, a celebration song of Momma's. A carriage comes our way, so I duck us back down in the woods, away from the strange cockeyed stare of the driver, his guns drawn. We hide until the horses rumble past. There is an awful lot of worry out on this road, isn't there? But I guess it's to be expected, on the way to the bandit town and everything.

We near the edge of the forest. The gates of Moon Haven are just ahead, tall and wooden and scarred, like they've kept out more people than they've let in. But today they are opened wide, just for me, and I'm so excited it takes all of me not to start running, to sprint through Moon Haven, straight to the Half-Moon Inn, straight to where I know my Gruff will be waiting.

But I don't. I wait till the last carriage passes, till it's just Tommy and me and the empty road. I put my hood down low over my face even though it's hot, just in case somebody might be able to spot me somehow. I stand out is all, with my hair and everything. Besides, you don't see two dirty kids wandering into a town alone too often. Especially not a town like Moon Haven.

The waiting is almost torture. The walls surround the whole town, and I can't see inside. I don't hear any music coming out of them. I don't smell any food either, just a weird charred smell, like a bonfire long gone out. A few men in hats stand outside the gates, smoking cigarettes, and that's about all. Maybe the fun stuff doesn't get started till night. If I know anything about bandits, they sleep late in the day and stay up late at night. That's what Gruff and the boys did anyway, until it was time for another job.

"This doesn't feel good," says Tommy. "I mean it. Everyone looks scared."

"They're probably just groggy from staying up too late and having too good a time," I say. "Now remember. Stay quiet and don't look anybody in the eye. I'm going to go see about getting a place to stay. You go buy us some food."

I hand him a few of Zeb's coins.

"Where am I going to get food?" he says.

"I don't know. There should be merchants and food carts and a market and all kinds of things. There should be food as far as you can see!"

"Think they'll have pie?" he says.

"I wouldn't doubt it. But you'll have to find a bakery for that."

"I bet we can buy us a whole pie," he says. "To celebrate."

"Any kind of pie you want," I say. "You ready?"

Tommy nods. I take a deep breath and walk out of the woods, through the gates into Moon Haven.

The streets are wide and muddy, mostly deserted. A few derelicts sleep on a street corner. Some dirty kids throw rocks at an orange cat. Most of the buildings are dark and quiet. Some have busted windows and their signs are hung crooked, the paint old and chipped. There's no parades, no dancing, just gloom, gloom everywhere. And for the life of me, I can't see any building big or grand enough to be the Half-Moon Inn. Not the way Gruff described it.

"There's a bakery," says Tommy. It's a small place, but the windows are lit, and people come and go carrying bread. Maybe there won't be any pies, nothing like that. But at least we'll have something to eat.

"Go be quick," I say. "We can meet back here in five minutes."

All of a sudden he's scared.

"Don't leave me alone, Goldeline."

"I'll be right back," I say. "Now go get us some grub."

He walks off toward the bakery, and I'm glad of it. Now I got to find Gruff.

An old lady sits on her front porch in a rocker. She's got a big wart on her nose, and one of her eyes squints. I'm scared of her but there's nobody else around, so I guess she'll do. I walk up to her and ask her in my sweetest little-girl voice like how I used to do on jobs, "Please, ma'am, can you tell me where the Half-Moon Inn is?"

"You come the same as all of us did, I wager. Young thing you are. Same as I was when I first come to Moon Haven."

"Please, ma'am. I have to meet a friend there. It's important."

The lady laughs. "Oh, I know how it is. You come expecting the lights, didn't you? You come expecting the artists, all the big murals, nothing but music everywhere, food and drink and laughing folks, that's what you expected. I can see it. I can see it all over your face." She spits on the porch boards. "I come looking for the same thing. Thirty years ago, at best. Don't look it now, but I was a right fair catch then. Secret was the foot."

The lady pulls up her skirts and there it is, plain as day, a foot carved right out of wood. She knocks on it.

"Hollow! Lost the real one in a poker game," she says. "Let me tell you, honey, don't ever bet your left foot on nothing, you hear me?"

"The Half-Moon Inn, ma'am. Can you tell me where it is?"

"That old dump? It's right over there," she says. "Or was, anyhow."

Dump? No, she can't be talking about the same place.

"It's not a dump," I say. "It's an inn. The biggest, most incredible inn in the whole world. Full of trapeze artists, and acrobats, and singers and . . ."

"I know, honey, I know," she says. "Those are the same stories they told me too, when I was your age. Doesn't matter anyhow. It's all gone."

The street's getting dark now, weird dusk time, when bats and night creatures come out, when long black cats stretch themselves in alleyways. The moon up there like a sad lady's face. This is Gruff's favorite time of night.

"I don't understand," I say.

"They burned it down," she says. "Just yesterday. Burned down the only place for people like us. Took the men out, flogged them in the street. No jail here, being a gambling town, a bandit town. So they tied them up. The gamblers, the magicians, the fortune-tellers, all of them. They . . . they . . ."

The old lady shuts her eyes, like she's gone weary all of a sudden, like she's about to keel over and faint.

"Who?" I say. "Who burned it down?"

"The Preacher," she says. "Come down from Templeton."

A cold hand grips my heart, all my songs gone quiet. As the lady talks I can see it in my mind, how the Preacher came to Moon Haven with torches all ablaze, shouting about judgment, he and his men charging in like demons. Flipping food carts, scattering the musicians all lined up in the streets, them tripping over their dresses, falling in the mud. The Preacher's men running behind them, laughing. He set fire to the Half-Moon Inn himself. But he would have said it was God's fire. He would have said that was God cleansing Moon Haven, like how fire's supposed to come down from the sky in the Great Reckoning and burn everything clean. Said he was doing the town a favor.

The lady dabs her eyes with her sleeve. "He didn't have to do that to folks just for being different, for not being perfect. Lord knows we all done things we weren't happy about. Hard to live any other way. Say, you okay there, little thing? What's a matter?"

I'm shaking and I can't see. All the tears I got in my face. I take off running, running toward the burning smell, running toward the center of town, toward the old oak tree sprouting high over the rooftops.

When I get to the charred black of earth that used to be the inn I feel sick. Fine things, a chandelier, jewelry, whatever's unburned glitters like fairy-book treasure in the dirt and rubble. The Preacher must have had an army to do this, a whole army of fanatics and followers, the Townies, his wicked congregation from Templeton.

But Gruff's too smart to get caught by them. Because real bandits don't get caught. Not my Gruff. Gruff would have heard them coming. He would have known it from a mile away. He would have slipped out back with a sack full of money and a jug of ale. Gruff got away, like he always does. I know it.

"Goldeline?" says a voice.

I whirl around, my heart so full of joy and hope. It's Gruff, it's Gruff, my Gruff made it out okay, he's alive.

But it isn't Gruff. It's only old Leebo, from the camp. I can't believe it. He's alive, somehow he got away.

"Thank the Lord, Goldeline, I thought you were dead," he says.

"Where's Gruff?" I say.

"I thought we'd lost you, Goldy. I was scared I'd never see you again."

Leebo balances on his crutch and opens his arms out wide for me to come and give him a hug, but I don't move.

"Leebo, where is Gruff?"

He bows his head a little.

"Well, darling . . ."

"Just tell me."

"They got him."

"But he's still alive, right? He's okay?"

Leebo shakes his head. He still won't look at me, he won't look me in the eyes, and I hate him a little bit for that.

"The Preacher hung him on the spot," he says. "Didn't even build a scaffold, just did it on that old oak tree right there. I saw it all. I was hiding in the crowd. He didn't holler, he didn't cower, he didn't say a word. He died good, Goldy."

I can't cry. I can't even talk. I can only watch the moon crawl up the trees and hang like a halo over the rubble.

This was supposed to be my home. I was supposed to live here with Gruff forever.

I sit down cross-legged in the dirt and Leebo sits down with me. We watch it get dark together, watch the stars come out over us. There's no mercy in this world. The stars are forever away. Gruff was wild and Gruff stole, but he stole to take care of me. He might have been wicked but he was mine, and he wasn't evil to me. He was the only one in the world that was any good to me at all.

An old woman in a long black robe walks up. She holds a little brass watering can in one hand and a tiny bell in the other. The woman makes a cross sign over the wreckage and begins to sing in a sad scratchy voice. Slowly she shuffles around the rubble of the Half-Moon Inn, singing all the while. Every few steps she sprinkles a little water on the ground and rings her bell.

"What's that lady doing, Leebo?" I say.

"She's a Mercy Woman," he says. "A holy woman."

"A preacher?"

"Not like the one who did this," says Leebo. "Mercy Women are different. They took care of my little brother once when he got sick, didn't ask for any money or nothing. They're like monks, but nicer. They show up whenever something real bad happens."

I wait until the old woman passes by again.

"What's that you're singing?" I say.

"It's a prayer," the woman says. She looks sad, but her eyes are bright and blue. "To heal this place from all the pain that has happened here."

"Aren't you afraid the Preacher will come back?" I ask her.

"No," she says. "I am old. What can that man do to me? As the Book says, 'Fear not the vain works of men. Fear not the darkness. For ye are creatures of light.' I sing here for healing on this land. No preacher can stop me from that."

She gets back to her slow singing work, and in my heart I'm grateful for her, that even in the worst moments there's always someone trying to do some good.

Me and Leebo sit there together a good long while watching the Mercy Woman work, until we hear voices in the night, men's voices in the street. I help Leebo up.

"Bye, Goldy," he says. "Take care of yourself." Leebo turns his head away from me and crosses over to the side of the street. "Trust me, it's safer if you stay away from me. He's after me, same as you. I won't do nothing but slow you down. Don't you come following me now."

"Wait!" I say, but he's turned a corner, he's gone now, like a stray cat scared and vanished off. That's probably how he didn't get caught, how he's managed to live so long as a bandit. I sit back down in the dirt to cry some more.

That's when Tommy comes running toward me, huffing, out of breath.

"Why'd you leave me?" he says. "I been looking everywhere

for you. We got to go, Goldeline. They know about us. The Preacher's been here. You won't believe all the kinds of stuff he said about us. They got us for assault and witchcraft and banditry and all kinds of things, stuff I never even heard of. And it isn't just you, Goldeline. It's me too. They know all about Zeb. The Preacher must have come back and found him. We got to hurry." He shakes me a little. "I said come on. We got to hurry."

I must have started crying again, because Tommy stops shaking me.

"What's wrong?" he says.

"They killed him," I say. "The Preacher killed Gruff."

He blinks at me like he can't believe it. Like he finally sees me for who I am.

"That's who you were taking us to? The thief?"

"He was the only person I had," I say.

"He was a bandit," says Tommy. "A real one. An evil man. He used you to rob people. Don't you understand that?"

"He loved me," I say. "He was my only one."

"No he wasn't," says Tommy. "You got me."

Men with lanterns are off in the distance, heading toward us.

"That's them," he says. "Goldeline, we got to go."

He looks taller now, braver somehow.

"Get up! They're going to kill us!"

"I don't care if they do," I say. "It was all a lie, Tommy. Everything Gruff told me about Moon Haven. All the stories he told me about the Half-Moon Inn."

Tommy looks at me real curious for a second.

"Too bad we didn't make it here in time," he says quietly. "It would have really been something to see."

"But don't you understand?" I say. "The stories weren't true. The Half-Moon Inn was just an old dump."

"How do you know?" he says. "You only saw it burned down, same as I did. Who knows what it looked like before then? I wouldn't doubt it was just the same as you told me it would be. I wouldn't doubt if it was even grander than in all the stories."

I gaze at Tommy a moment in wonder. It's like he understands something I don't, like he's reminding me of something I nearly forgot.

"I believe the stories you told me, Goldeline," he says. "I believe every word. Now we got to go."

The men are coming faster now, they've spotted us.

"Get up, Goldeline," he says. "Get up!"

Tommy yanks me up to my feet, and it's like he's pulling me out of a dream. Tommy's right. We can't get caught here, not like this.

An orange cat struts and stretches itself out on the busted boardwalk. I think it's the same one as before. It's looking right at me, eyes gold and aglow. *What do you say, kitty?* Its tail loops up like a question mark, and I know.

"This way," I say.

Tommy and me run to the closest storefront. The cat hops through a busted window smooth and quick as a ghost. The window is smashed and jagged with glass. I got to step careful through it. Tommy catches his knee on the glass and the skin rips and I think he's going to scream but he shuts his mouth and grimaces it down. The store inside is wrecked, a druggist's, little vials and bottles and powders all dark and horrible in the moonlight. It's a strange world the night gives you, when medicine bottles cast shadows like demons in every corner. Outside the men gather, peek through the busted window, their lanterns and torches shining at us. We clutch each other behind a shelf full of bottles and try to become as small as possible. I scoot us toward the back of the store and a bottle falls. It's just a tiny one, a hair tonic. Tommy reaches out to catch it but it tumbles off his fingers. The shatter makes every bone in me cringe.

The men heard it too. They bang on the door of the store, they kick until the lock breaks and they're inside and I know we're done for.

The orange cat looks up at me with her big eyes and shakes her head at me. She licks my palm, her tongue rough and hard, then meows her loudest.

No! I hiss. *Don't tell them where we are!*

The kitty looks back at me as if to smile, and struts toward the front of the store.

"Holy Lord, it's just a cat," says one of the men.

"Best not be using the Lord's name in vain," says another one. "Not while we're working for the Preacher anyhow."

"Shoot, he ain't here. He's off in the woods, hunting out escapees from the inn. He don't got a clue what we're doing."

"The Lord's got ears everywhere," says another. "That's what the Preacher says. The Lord's angels can hear everything you say, even everything you think. Then the angels come and whisper it right in his ear. That's what he says, anyhow."

"You believe him?"

"You seen what happens when folks don't believe him? They wind up dead. Shoot, if that's the case, I'll believe every word the man says."

"Well, either way, if we catch these two, it surely will get us on his good side. Like the Book says, cover a whole multitude of sins."

"It says 'Love covers over a multitude of sins,' idiot, not nabbing a couple of little kids."

"Whatever. Just so long as we're on his good side, I don't much care one way or the other about love."

They walk off down the road slow and careful, shining their lights in every window, searching for us. It's a strange thing, being hunted. I feel like my momma back on her death day, when they came by the house for her, when she sent me away to hide, when Gruff came and got me and brought me out to the woods.

When the men are good and gone, me and Tommy sneak back out the front door. Tommy limps a little from his knee but not much. When we pass the old oak I stop. I have to say good-bye to my Gruff.

I run over to where they hung him, under the branches of a tree older than all of us, a tree that will probably still be here long after we're all gone. I shut my eyes and try to see his face, try to look into his eyes and tell him I love him one last time. To thank him for saving me.

Sure, Gruff may have used me to help him steal. But that's just one way to tell the story, the way someone else might do it. In my story—the way I'll tell it until I die—Gruff saved my life. He showed me how to live in this world, what an evil place it could be and how to make it good anyhow. That's the way my story goes. And I dare anybody to tell me I'm wrong.

Good-bye, Gruff. I'll love you always in my heart and in my blood. I'll love you always with every one of my bones.

I blow him a kiss and let it fly up where his soul went, up to where the stars are. If love covers over a multitude of sins, then maybe Gruff's love for me saved him a little. It's worth a prayer.

Tommy grabs my hand and we run back down the street, back from where we came, back to the woods, not a hope left in the world for us except that we're two of us, together, not each one alone. Somewhere out there a wicked preacher waits, coiled up like a rattlesnake, fangs out and ready for us. He's hiding out there, and I hate thinking that we're running straight to him. But we got no choice. We run back into the long loud dark of the woods.

FIFTEEN

For maybe an hour me and Tommy stumble through the night. The moon is up high and ghosty, the clouds cracked like a mirror. It's hard to walk strange woods at night. You step and you're never sure where your foot will land, what vines can trip you, what clawing creatures hide themselves down in the dark.

I can't tell if we lost the men or not. Every few minutes I think I hear them behind us, a crackle and a stomp, a flicker of light where there shouldn't be any light. A fog's creeping up in the damp like there are demons on the prowl. We're tired and we're hungry and the night is dark and full of bird sounds, strange cracks and yips and breaks, what sounds sometimes like singing. It's like these woods are alive and full of ghosts tonight, wicked ones, the spirits of stranglers and child-nabbers huddled around cold fires. I know we made it safe through this forest once, just barely, but I'm scared to test my luck a second time. Tommy holds my hand and we walk through the woods with our other hands out like blind people, like kids scared of getting any more lost.

When we're too tired to go any farther I find us a tall tree with thick branches and a lot of leaves. It'll be good cover. We climb until we're higher than a man's head, up to a thick limb that forks just right for sitting. I hang my pack on a close-by branch where I can grab it easy if I need to. Tommy leans against the trunk and I lie back against him and he puts his arms around me, for safety. Even though it's hot I drape Zeb's momma's cloak over us, to protect us, to keep us hidden. Bats fly around, little blinks in the night. The moon is so lovely and unscared. She just shines and shines and wishes us well. I turn my face toward Tommy as best as I can. In the night his eyes are dark and glistening.

"Thanks, Tommy," I say. "You saved my life again."

"Happy to," he says, smiling. "I just can't wait till all this is over and we can get to my aunt Barbara's house."

"Yeah," I say. "You're really gonna love it there."

Soon Tommy's sleeping, his soft breath on my neck, his heartbeat gentle against my back, the warmth of the two of us together in the tree, safe and hidden.

I like being with Tommy, but it isn't the same. Tommy can't be my family. Not really. How can he be when all I can think about is Gruff, and always in my mind is Momma. My dead ones, the ones who loved me. They're the only family I'll ever have.

The tears start. I keep them quiet, lest I wake Tommy, lest I call the Preacher to us. I cry until I feel sleep coming. I hope I don't have any more dreams tonight. I hope I don't dream of Gruff. I don't think I could bear to wake up from it.

It's still dark night but I hear something, a cackle and a laugh from far off in the woods. Through the trees a little twig of smoke sticks out into the sky. People—a few men from the sounds of it—around a campfire.

I know I should stay up in the tree. I know it's too dangerous to climb down, to go searching, but I have to. Something tugs in me, a quiet whispering voice on the wind that latches into my heart and begs me forward. I loosen Tommy's arms from around me, careful not to wake him, and draw the cloak over my shoulders as I slide down the tree to the dirt below. I feel as if I'm in a dream, the soft flowing fog, the night birds, the lightning bugs blinking like green little souls.

It's so easy to be quiet when it's just me alone, no Tommy crashing around behind me. Barefoot on the soft soil, I take myself through the fog, led by the breeze as if it were a song only I can hear. The moon looks down with a question in its eye. I'm on a mission, I know that, woken up just for this purpose. I creep close to the ground and quiet as a cat to the campfire. Three men lie sleeping around it, with four more sitting up, their backs hunched down, facing the fire. A soft-singing voice hums quiet, and it takes me a minute to know the song, but I do. It's a hymn.

The voice is one I know too, from real life and from nightmares. It's the Preacher.

"Right fearful night," says one of the other men. "Could be all sorts of bandits afoot."

The Preacher stops singing.

"Worse things in these woods than mere bandits," he says. He chuckles to himself. "No, I'd reckon bandits are the least of our fears."

"What you getting at, Preacher?" says the other man. "It's just kids we're chasing."

"Kids, yes, from first look. Kids just like any other. Could be your very own children, your nieces and nephews. Evil loves to take a form of innocence, of beauty. Even a child."

"You saying these kids is under the grip of the Evil One?" says the other man.

"Inside them lie dark and malign forces, set against us," says the Preacher. He speaks slowly, softly, like he's reciting. "The girl has a forked tongue. Her words are venom, a false gospel, rot to your ears. She will enchant you. Same as she enchanted the boy. She bent him, twisted him fiendish, made him crooked and as wretched as herself. He's lost to us."

The smoke from the fire is a black curtain toward the

woods that I can't see past. It's as if the fire itself is talking. When it wafts away I see the Preacher sitting up on a log, his back stooped, his silhouette a giant black crow.

"How'd she get like that? I mean, how did a devil come to this girl we're hunting?" says the third man.

"Her mother," says the Preacher. "Her mother was a witch. One of the first we cleansed, back in Templeton, in the early days of our revival, when the Lord first gave me the words with which to heal this land. A spirit of witchcraft may enter a child many different ways, by blood, by ritual. Sometimes the spirit even passes into a child through the bottoms of her feet, the tenderest place, while the babe is still in her mother's womb. Such a child is doomed before she is born. So it is with the girl we're chasing. She is her mother's daughter, through and through, from the white hair to the gold of her eyes. Every bit her mother."

I hate when the Preacher talks about Momma. I hate that his words can touch her, can call her face up in my mind, can put her face over mine. That's not his right. I creep around the edge of the campsite, so I can see them better. The Preacher spits into the fire. His hands twist a long blade of grass around his finger, twirling and untwirling it, tight then loose, in a spiral. He is working his magic over them, casting his enchantment with words. When he speaks it's like I can see the words dangle and twirl in the air, dancing through the night and smoke and fire, bewitching the men, holding sway over their hearts and minds.

"What do you know about evil?" says the Preacher. "From whence does evil come?"

"You mean how folks go wrong?" says the other man.

"I mean how evil *begins*. It starts small, tiny and quick as a notion, a pinch on bare skin, a stray spark in the cold darkness, that's what evil is. But it isn't content to be a spark, a pinch, a notion. A notion begets an idea, a plan. Just as a pinch begets a touch, flesh on flesh, a caress. And a spark always begets a flame."

The Preacher stretches his hands over the fire, spreads his fingers wide, the gangling spindly talons of them. The fire glows his hands red, glimmers his teeth. His scar shines like a seam, a stitching place healed over wrong.

"It's an ancient story, the very first one in all the Book. The Great Garden at the Beginning of the World. Perfection was a trial and man failed it. But the problem wasn't man. It is the nature of man to fail such a test, creature that he is, lit alive by desire. Dangle the wicked fruit before a man and every time he will pluck it. The problem isn't us. The problem is the fruit—tender, red-rotten, the tempting fruit. The garden is vast, and the trees are many. As the Book says, 'Find the tree which beareth the tempting fruit. Uproot it and let it burn. Lest the evil sow its seed, lest the evil cause itself to spread, lest the garden be overwhelmed.'

"You remember how it was in Templeton, even just a

couple years ago," says the Preacher. He spreads his arms wide and his shadow casts a cross, crooked and long, his fingers stretched into the darkness. His words wild dancing things that swirl through the air, bedeviling the men. "Bars and gambling, murder and crime, the disease. Homes wrecked and ruined. The woods of bandits on the left-hand side, a cursed forest on the right, our good and faithful town of Templeton stuck right in the midst of them. Every nightfall brought a new terror, did it not? You remember how afraid you were. Isn't it better now?"

The Preacher claps his hands together. His white hair wild, his hat wide-brimmed, his face ghastly and firelit, like a devil conjured up just for this meeting, this purpose and this reckoning. The smoke from the fire trembles away from him, as if it were afraid.

"You're right about that, Preacher," says the other man. "Templeton ain't even the same town anymore. Folks are safe now. My wife don't worry about a thing. Only thing my kids are afraid of is snakes. Ain't a bit like it used to be."

"And you, Bolivar Greencoats," says the Preacher, and I can't believe it. There he is, Mr. Greencoats, the man me and Gruff robbed and set loose in the woods, a man given my own forgetting herbs. He sits by the fire, low-down and squat and afraid. "Do you not remember the state in which I found you? Do you not recall the way you blathered and blubbered, mind gone blank and eyes baffled wide, the confusion on your face? You could not recall the names of your children, Bolivar Greencoats, you could not recall the face of your mother. You, wandering the forest like a lost son of the desert, half naked and wild. I healed you, I set you free from the little witch girl's enchantments. Do you recall what I have done for you?"

"Yes sir," says Mr. Greencoats. I can see the fear in his eyes. The fear of what I did to him, and the fear of the Preacher's own power, a magic every bit as dark as anything he accused me and Momma of.

"These children are seed sowed by bad fruit," says the Preacher. "They will grow, and they will become unwieldy. They will spread their evil throughout the land, their blasphemy, their witchcraft, until the land is overcome. Yes, and then they will ravage. Do you now understand why we must catch them?"

"Yes sir," says the third man. "I reckon I do."

Is the town really safer now that Momma is dead? Now that Gruff and his boys are killed? The Preacher might be right. Maybe we were bad for the town. Me and Gruff robbed so many people. In my ears I hear every terrified scream of them.

"Wish we would have brought all the other guys, too," says the third man. "Wish we hadn't left them back in Moon Haven, while we're out hunting something so fierce as devils made flesh."

"Hard to run an army through a forest," says the Preacher. "We can move quiet, just the few of us. We can find her and the boy faster this way. The Evil One is cunning, both serpent and lion, always on the prowl. We must be sober, and we must be vigilant. The Lord is our strength. He won't let us fail."

"Still," says the third man. "Wish there were more of us anyhow."

"Get your sleep," says the Preacher. "Come God's blessed dawn we got demons to send home. Regis has this hour's watch, don't you?"

"Yes sir," says the other man. "Couldn't sleep a lick after all this devil talk anyhow."

"He shall grant his children tender sleep," says the Preacher, lying down. "And the Lord is good to his word."

"I hope so," says the third man, lying down as well. "Hate gotdang nightmares."

Regis, the man on watch, clutches his rifle and looks toward the fire. There's a big gleaming knife laid out on a rock by his side. I wait just outside the firelight, belly to the ground, my body hidden by the fog, for what seems like hours. I feel like a cat tracking a bird. My eyes are sharp in the night, I can see extra close, I can see the stubble on the watchman's chin, I can smell his breath from the flask he sips out of once he thinks the Preacher is asleep. And the Preacher is asleep, far as I can tell. His chest rises and falls steady like, in a rhythm. All I have to do is wait for Regis to sleep too.

I watch that knife, how it calls to me, how I got to revenge Momma and revenge Gruff, revenge myself. I feel it in my bones, my blood, the readiness that comes from fear. I am quiet and cool, coiled tight, a snake ready to pounce. I just have to wait for the perfect moment. I can wait for hours and hours. For the moon to be covered by clouds and the night to become dark, too dark for anyone to see except creatures like me, like the owls, us hunters in the dark. For Regis to take one too many nips from his flask. For his eyes to droop, for his head to nod, for it to bob like a cork in the water and then sink finally, chin to chest, until I know he is good and asleep.

I sneak up so soft I could be a death angel's whisper. I don't even rustle a leaf, I leave no tracks, I'm the Ghost Girl of the Woods, the demon-possessed, the one they've all heard stories about.

I snatch the knife from off the rock. It's heavy in my hand. The power of it is wonderful, to carry all this death in my little palm. The fire-glow glints off the blade in daggers of light that slice the night clear. An owl swivels his head around to peek at me, eyes bright as stars. I creep on all fours over to the Preacher. He sleeps on his back, his mouth shut in a slit of a grin. His face is clean-shaven, eyebrows black, with a long scar from his left eye socket down his cheek, like the path of a tear, like it's his skin that's been crying.

I raise the knife over him in both my hands. I say the words in my heart, like a silent prayer. *This is for Gruff. This is for the Half-Moon Inn, my dreams burned down to rubble. This is for sending me out to the woods to be a bandit, to steal from good folks. Most of all, this is for my momma.*

But just before I plunge the knife, Bobba's voice screams inside my head. Just one word, so loud it makes me deaf to everything but itself.

Remember!

It stops me cold, the knife over my head, the fire crackling just to my side. The moon uncovers itself and sends a white beam right onto the Preacher's face so that it glows.

The Preacher opens his eyes.

The look on his face, of terror and sadness, his ghost-haunted eyes, a pain so violent I can almost hear it screaming.

I remember. I do. I remember every single awful bit of it.

I drop the knife and stumble backward. I crawl my way into the fog. The Preacher jerks awake, jumps to his feet, and trips over again.

"Wake up!" he says. "She's here! Up, you fools! The girl is here!"

But I'm running already. Tree branches swing at me like hooks, roots rise up to trip me. Mosquitoes buzz in my ears and all the lightning bugs shut off their lights. It's like the whole forest is against me, like I've stumbled into a place gone spoiled by wickedness. I have to get back to the tree. I have to warn Tommy. I have to wake him and get him out of here. He can't die because of me. I won't let him. The fog hides my feet, it's like wading in a ghostly river, dead fish nipping at my toes. I was a fool to try and kill the Preacher, to lift the knife to him. Because that wasn't my mission, that wasn't the reason I was woken up and sent into the night, I know that now, I knew it the moment I looked into his eyes and saw what I saw. My mission wasn't to kill the Preacher. It was to remember.

I climb the tree and clap my hand over Tommy's mouth. He wakes with a start and we both almost topple out. But I hold him tight, I hold us both up there together. I hold my finger to my lips and whisper, "He's out there." The Preacher and his men crashing around, breaking branches, scaring all the sleeping creatures awake.

The clouds slide over the moon again, giving us back the dark. I grab my pack, and Tommy and me slip down the tree and take off in the quietest run we can. The fog is still thick, we bump into trees, branches claw at our faces, we trip and stumble. Behind us are the torches of the Preacher's men glowing like eyes off in the night. The Preacher screaming for his men to run, to find us.

We hit on a path. It's small but mostly clear, without tree limbs reaching out to block us. We can move quicker here, and I let Tommy's hand go. We run together in a full-on sprint, away from the voices, away from the Preacher and his death. Their lights get smaller and smaller with every glance backward.

"We're gonna make it," I say, my voice gravelly, panting, out of breath. I look back at him and smile. "We're gonna get away."

That's when Tommy trips.

It must have been a root, something my foot didn't catch. His feet leave the ground and he lifts up like he's a bird taking off into the air. But Tommy doesn't rise. He falls hard, his face smacking the dirt, tumbling off the path, down a hill it's too dark to see the bottom of, into some kind of ditch where he vanishes into the fog. I hear a snapping sound and the long wailing howl of pain.

I could keep running. If I hustle, if I don't stop for anything, I could make it, I could get away. But Tommy's my best friend, I know that now, the only true friend I've ever had. Whatever happens, I love Tommy. I love him and I can't leave him here. I take a deep breath and dive right into the fog after him.

I slide on my knees down a hill, into some sort of a gully. I follow his moaning, groping with my hands until I find Tommy. I clap my hand over his mouth, his tears sliding hot over my fingers, and hold him as tight as I can.

"I'm sorry, Tommy," I tell him. "I'm so, so sorry. Shhhh. I shouldn't have let go of your hand. Shhhh. I'm so sorry. We have to be quiet now. We have to be quiet."

He shakes with pain. I feel the stickiness of blood down by my feet. Tommy lets out a whimper and goes slack in my arms, like he's dead. But I can still feel his breath on my hand. He's not dead, he's not. I start to let my hand off his mouth, to go down to his leg and see if I can bind up whatever is cut, whatever is hurt, whatever is broken on him, when I hear the sound of footsteps on the path, not five feet away from us, the whisper of voices.

I hold Tommy close and burrow silently down into the leaves and pray the fog covers us like a blanket. I shut my eyes so no light catches them. I refuse to breathe, to think. I will my heart to stop beating, scared the Preacher will hear even that.

His footsteps are so close. I can feel the heat from his torch, hear it flicker and pop.

"Come on out, little one," he says. "You've been running from me for so long. You don't have to run anymore."

I can feel his eyes on me. I can hear his tired breathing. He is so close now I could reach out and touch him, I just know it. But I do not dare open my eyes. I do not dare so much as turn my head toward him. He would know it. The wickedness in him would know I was there.

"Come to me, little one. Do not be afraid. You know me now, don't you? You know who I am again. I saw it in your eyes. This day has been long coming, since well before your mother died and you ran from me. The Lord has been preparing us for this day. I couldn't take you before, but you know now, and it is time. These past seven years He has raised you and me up for this very purpose. It will be decided. Surrender yourself."

He is so close now I can feel his breath on my cheek. I want to go. I want to stand up and give myself in.

I could leave Tommy hidden. I could ransom myself for him, get the Preacher off his trail. I could save Tommy easy, just by giving in, by standing up right now, by letting the Preacher have me. It would be so easy.

But then come other footsteps, loud, hollering voices.

"You find her, boss?" says a voice. It's Regis.

"I wouldn't have lost her had you been awake."

"I'm sorry, Preacher."

"You reek of intemperance," he says. "You stink of dissipation."

"I'm awful sorry, Preacher. I just got scared."

"Shut your mouth."

The other men come running up, tired, panting and out of breath.

"Look everywhere," says the Preacher. "They can't have gotten far."

But the spell is broken. The hold he had on me is gone. His voice is magic, like a river current, drawing me always to him. No wonder he hoodwinked all the Townies. The Preacher almost had me too. He almost got me to give in.

The Preacher and his men head along down the path, searching for us. When they're gone I drag Tommy out of the fog and into the tiniest sliver of moonlight. I just want to see his leg, what's happened to it. His foot is twisted, the ankle snapped. His pants cuff is covered in blood. I lift it just a little and see bone jutting through his skin like teeth.

I tear the hem off his momma's dress and tie it tight around his foot. I have to get him to a doctor. I have to get him to someone who can help.

In the long distance I see torches. It's too dangerous to move now. I only pray Tommy can make it through the night.

I pull him back down into the ditch, careful not to hurt his ankle any more. I'm thankful he stays passed out. I cover him with leaves until I can't hardly even see his face. Then I burrow myself down in there with him, as hidden as we possibly can be.

I'm afraid. Because I know why the Preacher hates me, why he hated my momma so bad he had to kill her. I know why he came back for us. I know what Bobba drugged me for, what she wanted so bad for me to remember. What Momma tried so hard to make me always forget.

See, I remembered. I remember everything.

SIXTEEN

That night at the window, the strange man in all black, the wild white hair, his back to me. I see it all now. The memory loops itself in my head like a bad path that doubles back and leaves you in a circle. I see it brighter and clearer every time.

I'm at the window of Momma's house and I'm five or four years old and I'm peeking in like I'm not supposed to, it isn't time yet. There he is, the stranger, the man in black clothes with the white hair. But this time I can hear him. This time I know him, just from the music of his voice. It's the Preacher.

He isn't saying awful stuff to Momma though. He isn't spitting at her or screaming at her either like he did when he took her away.

"I love you," he says. "I love you with all my heart and

guts, with my mind and bones. The blood in me loves you."

The Preacher falls to his knees. His body slumps, his coat drags in the dust, his eyes are soft and blue. He takes her hand and rubs it on his cheek. He kisses her fingers.

"Please love me," he says. "If it be my undoing, please love me. If it be my ruin, please love me. If I lose my seat at the Banquet at the World's End when the sky has turned to fire and the earth closed in on itself, if I'm condemned forever in the Great Reckoning, cast into the darkness always, please love me."

On his knees in Momma's tiny little cabin, the Preacher weeps. Big animal tears, sobs like hacking coughs.

He kisses the hem of her dress, wipes his tears on it. He clutches at her feet and buries his face in them. He kisses them. He calls her his beautiful, his precious, his only.

"No one has to know who you are, what you've been," says the Preacher. "We can start all over."

Momma's eyes flash, and a sad smile crawls over her face.

Momma steps back away from the Preacher. He's on the ground now, flat on his face. Momma's got her fake-angry voice on, like when she used to play games, like when she used to tease me. She crouches down and her white dress covers her like angels' wings. She lifts his face with her finger and looks him in the eyes.

"What kind of man of God are you, Cyrus? To be out here in the middle of the night, proposing to someone like me?"

"We could leave here together," he says. "Take Goldeline with us. We could have us a good life, where no one knew us. We could start over. It could be the three of us. A family."

A family, he said.

I remembered the Preacher coming now. Mr. Cyrus was what I was supposed to call him, Mr. Cyrus Cantor. How he sat me on his lap and read me storybooks. That's how I know the Book so well. He used to bring it home from the reliquary and read it to me himself. All the best stories, about the strong man and the sad wife, the flooding and the endless night, the idol and the dragon, the she-bears and the bald man. He played with me. He was like my daddy. Before Gruff, before anybody. He would come at night when no one knew. Mr. Cyrus was good to me.

"I can't, Cyrus. I'm a witch, and you know it," she said. "We aren't bound to anyone except our own kind. More than that, I don't want to get married. I don't want to be anybody's wife."

"But how could you want things to be wrong?" he says. "I can't be with you any other way except married. That's the only way you and me can be good. That's the only way it'll be right. Don't you understand?"

"I think I'm starting to, Cyrus," she says, "and I don't like it."

"If it's the only good thing you ever do," he says, "please marry me. Be my wife. Make things right, with me and with yourself and with God. Let's start a life together, a daylight life, one out in the open for anyone to see."

My momma, face flushed red, gold-flecked fire in her eyes, hair soft white billowing out about her like some crazy wind rushed through the house, so beautiful I almost have to shut my eyes against it. Momma looks the Preacher dead in the eyes.

"You're a good man, Cyrus. You've been so good to me, and to Goldeline. But you can't go marrying me. Not with you being a preacher, not with me being what I am. You put a chain on me and I'd turn to ash in your hands. I'd rather be dead than married. It's just the truth. I'm a witch, Cyrus, and I don't belong to anyone except myself."

"But you're not like other witches I've heard about," he says. "All the stories of evil and wickedness folks tell. You help people. You heal them, you don't curse them."

Momma hooks an eyebrow at Mr. Cyrus, and a look comes over her that I've never seen before. Something dark and mysterious in her eyes, and for a moment she doesn't look at all like the Momma I know.

"Are you sure I haven't cursed anybody, Cyrus?" she says. "Maybe I never hurt anyone in Templeton, but what about long ago, before I got here? How do you know I haven't sent rot over a neighbor's cornfield just because he was mean to me, or made some old lecher's face blister with boils? How do you know I haven't cursed a liar mute, or turned a cruel man's cup of wine to blood? You have no idea what I've done, Cyrus. You don't know where I've been, what I had to do to survive. You don't know what I've done just for the sheer pleasure of it."

Mr. Cyrus puts his face in his hands and cries. I never seen a grown person cry like that, shake and moan. I can't help but feel bad for him, how he has to love Momma in his own way, how he can't love her in her way. It's no good to make Momma marry. Even I know that. She's not that kind, never could be, never would want to be. But I never heard of Momma cursing anyone before. Her magic was always good. I never knew she could do a thing like that.

"You don't know what it's like," he says. "You don't know what it feels like to ache and burn like this, to want something so bad it kills you."

"You think I don't know what it's like to want things?" says Momma. "You think I don't want a better life for my girl than this? Out here in the woods, away from everything, barely eating every week?"

"Then come with me," says Mr. Cyrus. He's on his knees, pleading. "Marry me. Be with me forever."

"I can't do that, Cyrus. You know that."

"But I need you," he says. "And Goldeline needs a father." Mr. Cyrus looks at Momma, his eyes flinting in the firelight. "I've seen her, you know. I've seen what happens when Goldeline sings that song you taught her, the way it speaks pictures into my mind. I've seen her conjure, even if she didn't know she was doing it. I've seen her call a wind to snuff out candles while she's sleeping. I've seen a doe kneel down to her in the woods while she let her pet it. I know Goldeline's every bit the witch you are, and I can prove it."

"What are you saying, Cyrus?"

"I'm saying folks will be mighty interested to know what kind of daughter you're raising. What kind of danger you're putting their kids in, letting her hang around them. I'll tell them everything. Unless you marry me. Unless you come and live with me in town, be my wife."

Momma's mad now. I can see a fire start in her, right down at her toes, and rise slowly up. She balls her fists, all her power and pride and anger sliding up into her face, sparking her eyes.

"No, Cyrus," she says. "My answer is no. Get out of my house, and don't you dare ever come back."

The Preacher screams something awful. He pounds his fists on our floor, the veins bright purple on his face, bulging. He screams again. Momma puts her hand to her cheek, like she's scared, like she knows maybe she went too far this time.

"Cyrus?" she says.

She reaches out and lightly touches his head.

The Preacher slaps her hand away. He crawls toward her and grabs her dress. Momma tries to run but he yanks her down. She claws at Mr. Cyrus's eye, her fingernails ripping a gash down his cheek.

It's like something breaks inside of me, like whatever ghost had clapped its hand over my mouth is gone.

I scream, loud and hard as I can. I scream with every bit of strength I got.

The Preacher turns to the window, eyes red-lined, face fierce and ugly as a demon.

When he sees me his scowl softens, his eyes go blue again, they stare straight into me, a look of awful sadness I'll never forget, the very same look that brought these memories back to me again. Great big tears stream down his cheeks. He looks down at his hands and moans, a horrible leg-broke-dog howl.

"Goldeline?" says Momma, her voice gone ragged.

I'm scared the Preacher's coming for me, but he doesn't. He runs to his horse and he climbs onto it and he rides away from us, away from Templeton, into the woods. And we wouldn't see him again for years and years, and even then I wouldn't remember.

I run inside and hold my momma while she cries. I cover her with my own body. I hold her and I kiss her eyes and I let her hold me too.

When she can sit up I help her. She tells me to get her certain things, roots and leaves, weird stuff she uses in her healings, and bring them to her. Some I have to go out and pick. It takes me all night but I do it. Every few minutes I come in and check on her and she seems a little better, a little less upset each time. It's a miracle, what my momma can do. It's her magic.

When I have all the ingredients and the sun is just breaking the trees and turning the dark world soft again, she bids me build her a fire and I do. We fill the cauldron with water, and I watch my momma drop in each powder, each leaf and root, singing all the while, singing each magic word in a language I don't know, lovely as birdsong.

The smell fills the room, a sick oily dead smell, the worst I ever sniffed. She's making tea from the forgetting herbs, same as what I would do for Gruff years later. Momma taught me this magic, it's the only thing of hers I still have with me, the only magic she let me keep. I guess that's why Momma never taught me any more of it. She was trying to protect me from men like the Preacher.

"Taste this," Momma says, holding a big spoonful toward me.

I don't want to. It smells awful, it smells like death and rot. But she grabs me by the hair and yanks my head back and my mouth opens and she plunges the spoon in. Then another and another. I gag and choke, it burns my mouth, it tastes yucky, my eyes go black. I almost vomit it up but Momma holds her hand over my mouth.

"Swallow it," she says, and I do.

My stomach swirls and my hands tingle and I feel dizzy. Momma carries me over to the bed and sits me down on it. She kneels in front of me. I almost topple over but she holds me up with both her hands.

"Open your eyes," she says.

"But, Momma, I can't."

"Open your eyes."

I can hardly see her. Everything is hazy and soft, the white of the light through the window, fuzzy as cat fur.

"Say what I say."

"Yes, Momma."

"Last night was all a dream."

"Last night was all a dream."

"Mr. Cyrus was never here."

"Mr. Cyrus was never here."

"It was all a bad dream."

"Just a dream."

"There's no Preacher coming to see us again. Never has been."

"No Preacher, never has been."

"You never saw that man once before in your whole life."

"Never saw anybody."

"Your momma loves you more than anything. She's never gonna let anything happen to you."

"Momma loves me more than anything. Nothing bad will happen to me."

"That's my Goldy," she says, and pulls me to her. We lie down together on the bed and while she kisses my hair and cries soft so as not to wake me, I think, *This is all a dream, this is just a dream, none of this ever happened*, until all I see is nothing and all I hear is nothing and finally I'm asleep.

SEVENTEEN

ootsteps crunch the leaves beside my head. I don't know how I fell asleep, how the memory became a dream again. But there are boots beside me, a man with a bald head peering down at me.

"Well, what do we got here?" he says.

I grab Tommy across his chest and pull him to me. He mumbles to himself, fever-hot, yelling at folks in his dreams.

"Your friend don't look too good," the man says. "Might better let me take a look at him."

I shake my head no, and when the man tries to grab at Tommy I snap my teeth at his fingers. He yanks his hand back and laughs a little.

"You are a mighty tough one, aren't you? Have to be, to survive out here in these woods. Especially with certain folks afoot. Unwanted folk, prowling around here, if you know what I mean."

Again I shake my head no and growl at him. He'll have to kill me if he wants to take Tommy. I don't trust anybody anymore. The whole world is full of wretched and evil people and even the ones you love like your own momma aren't perfect, they can be mean and cruel even if they don't deserve at all what comes to them. My momma with her face all angry, the Preacher crying on his knees, kissing her fingers. Not a lick of it do I understand. Not one bit at all.

The man bends down and squints his eyes at me. His eyebrows crinkle up, fat as caterpillars.

"I don't expect you to trust me. Heck, I wouldn't much trust myself out here. But your friend's got a break in his ankle. A bad break. The bone is poking through. Now you could stay out here, have him lose the foot, maybe his whole leg. Shoot, might be too late for him already. Or you can help me get him back to my place, have ol' Chester take a look at him. He ain't any doctor or anything, but in my experience a not-doctor sometimes can out-doctor a real doctor, if you follow me."

I think maybe I kind of do. That's what my momma was when she healed people. A good not-doctor. She helped babies and pregnant women and old ladies with hands crumpled up like claws. Momma could soothe them, could make their fingers spread out again. She knew all kinds of things. But I still don't trust this man. I don't know anything about him.

"My name is Lance," he says. "And I'm trying to save your friend's life. Do you understand? If you stay here, your friend will die. But if you come with me, he might can live. Hustle and we maybe could even save the leg. Besides," he says, cutting a glance around the woods, "some folks have been knocking on doors, looking for a couple of kids out here in the wild. Saying they're bandits, demon-possessed. Now y'all wouldn't want to be out here with any demon-bandit children running around, would you?"

He winks at me, and maybe he knows. The morning is black, clouds scowling at the earth. A cardinal looks down from the trees and tilts his head at me, like he wants to know what I'm going to do.

"Who's Chester?" I say.

"Oh, you'll like him. You'll like him fine. I think you and Chester will wind up mighty tight friends, if you ask me." He looks up at the darkening sky and sighs. "Look, we ain't got time to talk. You coming or not?"

Tommy's hands move in jerks. He's chomping his teeth, fighting out against some fever demon. His eyelids flutter open and shut, his pupils rolled back so all I can see is white. He looks bad, real bad. I'm scared.

"Okay," I say, "we'll go."

"First you got to help me rig up a splint for him. And we

got to keep him from hollering out too much, if you don't mind." Lance spits in the dirt and toes it with his boot. "What I mean is, this sucker's going to hurt. Do what you can for me."

Tommy's a little bit awake now, coming in and out, yelping when we jostle him too much. Lance braces his leg with two sticks and begins wrapping it tight with cloth. Tommy screams and his face gets redder and redder. I kiss his cheeks and sing to him one of Momma's songs, the one my momma used to sing me whenever I got sick. *There's no healing without music*, she used to say. *Music gets way down past your blood, past your bones even. It gets into the dark of you, where you're sickest of all. You got to sing all the sick away. You got to fill your darkest places full of light.*

"That's a pretty song," says Lance.

"My momma taught it to me," I say.

"Then that's just the right song to sing."

It takes us a minute to get Tommy to where we're holding him up. Lance isn't all that much taller than me, so it works out okay.

"Let's move quick," says Lance, "but smooth if we can manage it. Only about a mile to my place if we keep off the roads. Just watch your step and let's try not to hurt the boy too much."

It takes us a good half hour. Twice we almost fall, and twice Tommy howls like we stuck him with a fire poker. But we never do go all the way down, and pretty soon, grunting and sweating and huffing, we get to a cabin in a small bit of clearing off the road.

"Home sweet hovel," says Lance. "And thank the Lord, because I'm wore out. I ain't worked this hard since I was a farm boy, and I flat hated that junk. Now let's get the boy some help, shall we?"

The cabin is bigger than mine and Momma's was, with a good roof and a chimney puffing smoke. There's a garden out front, full of purples and blues, with an apple tree dangling bright reds. It's a happy house, I think. It looks like happy people live here. A white kitty with a black tail rubs itself against the door like it wants to come in. Maybe it wants us all to come in too.

What do you say, kitty?

The door opens before we even have time to knock. A straggly-haired man who is maybe sixty bends down and strokes the kitty's back. "Hi there, Princess," he says. "Princess Mona." Then he sees us. "My little Mona, what have you brought us today?"

"Chester, it ain't the cat that drug this boy out from the ditch," says Lance. "Just me and this one here. What'd you say your name was?"

"Goldeline," I say. It feels good to say my name out loud. It feels like I lit a little candle inside myself again.

"Goldeline," says Chester. "Such a pretty name."

"Thank you," I say, and I mean it. It's been so long since someone said something really truly nice to me.

"And who is this little bird you've brought me?"

"His name's Tommy," I say. "And his ankle's broke up real bad."

"I see," says Chester, bending down to look at Tommy's splint.

"Think you can help him?"

"Darling, I shall do my part. That I promise you," he says, with a little bow. Princess Mona rubs herself against my leg, purring. I like Chester, I think. Him and Lance both.

"Great. Now let's get the little guy inside," says Lance. "I'm about sick to death of carrying him and my shoulder's liable to give out."

"Old man," laughs Chester.

"Shoot," says Lance. "Ain't any older than you are."

We follow Chester into the house. It's lovely, clean, and bright with life. Flowers cut and arranged in vases, a warm fire, and a big grand table. A painting of an old man on the wall, with a little girl holding some flowers. And best of all, books and books, shelves full, on the floor, piled up everywhere, a whole fortune of books. We lay Tommy on the table.

"Where are we?" says Tommy.

"You're at our home," says Chester. "I'm going to try and fix up your leg a little bit. How does that sound?"

"Sounds like it's gonna hurt," says Tommy.

"Unfortunately, you're right about that," says Chester. "But we'll do what we can. Goldeline? Can you get me that bottle over there?"

He points to a big green glass with a cork stuck in it. I get it from the table, but when I bring it near Tommy he gets scared.

"Don't make me drink anything," he says.

I won't give Chester the bottle until he tells me what it is.

"We got poisoned by an old lady named Bobba," I explain. "She lived in a tree."

"Ah," he says. "Well, no poison here. Just something to calm the boy down. See?" He takes the bottle from me and uncorks it. He takes a swig of it himself, then holds it out to me to sniff. It doesn't smell evil. This place is different than Bobba's. It's a good home. There isn't any magic here except the kind that comes from goodness. It's a warmth that fills me all over.

"It's safe," he tells Tommy. "But it won't taste real good, so pinch your nose."

Tommy does and Chester gives him a glug. Tommy coughs, and Chester makes him drink again.

"I feel kinda loopy," he says.

"Good," says Chester. "Then I guess we're ready to start."

It takes a lot of blood to set the bones right. The cut is nasty, blue with infection. Tommy screams and cries, even with the medicine. Lance brings cool rags for Tommy's head. He's screaming so loud. I'm scared he's going to die.

"Sing him one of your songs," says Lance.

So I do. I sing him the nothingsong. It's wordless, but I sing a story into it this time. I figure maybe I should be sick of stories by now, with all the trouble they've gotten me into. But I don't think stories are good or bad in themselves. It's like the way the Preacher uses the Book—and all the strange and confusing and lovely things in it—for evil, when its stories can be used just as easy for good. Or the way Gruff lied to me about Moon Haven, how bad it hurt me when I found out. But maybe Gruff's stories weren't lies, not really. Maybe they were just the truth about how things should be, how maybe a derelict little orphan girl like me needed a place like the Half-Moon Inn he dreamed up for me. Maybe sometimes the story is more about the teller, and the hearer too, than ever it is about the story itself.

I sing Tommy the story of what the nothingsong has always been to me. About a ghost girl, a girl from the moon. She came down just a tiny thing, no bigger than a fleck of starlight. She was born on earth in a cut of sugarcane. A farmer found her one day and brought her home to his wife. They raised the little ghost girl until she was normal-person-sized and the prettiest girl in all the land. Kings and princes and lords and merchants from all over the world came to woo her, but she didn't like a one of them. They all smelled bad or talked about politics or bored her with stories of killing wolves and tigers, stories that the girl wished had ended with the tigers and wolves winning, stuffing their bellies full of these awful men.

But there was one boy, barely sixteen, who rode into the ghost girl's village. He had silver hair and walked with a cane, but the cane had a sword in it. He didn't bore her talking about all the stuff he killed, or about what was happening at court and all that other junk. Instead, he sang her a song. And the song was the story of her whole life, only said quicker and more beautiful than she could have ever said it herself. The music and the words and the young man's voice, all of it together scooped her heart up and took it away. It was the singing boy she would marry.

It didn't work though. Just when it was time for the wedding ceremony, the ghost girl's parents came back from the moon. They said she had to come back home. The moon missed her, it needed her light, there wasn't anybody else in the whole starry night that could give enough glow to the moon. It had to be her.

So she waved good-bye to the boy she loved and to her earth parents and floated up into the sky, and that was that.

Sure, the song doesn't have any words to it. But that's what it's about. Anyone with a half a brain can tell that. What else could a song so beautiful be about except a ghost girl and her journey to the moon?

When I finish singing, I realize that everybody's looking at me. Tommy's eyes seem soft, and there isn't a mark of pain in his face. Chester looks at me with wide blue eyes, stitches and thread still in his hand. Lance sits quiet in the corner. All from my little song. Maybe Momma left me a little more magic than I thought.

"Please sing it again," says Chester.

And I do.

Soon Tommy's leg is all stitched up and he's snoozing soft and snoring. Lance has been cooking, and he serves up a big beef stew that smells wonderful, that doesn't have any beets in it or bad magic. It's real food, rich and thick. We eat and eat and eat.

"Is Tommy gonna be okay?" I ask.

"Looks like it, darling," says Chester. "You did a miracle by singing like that. It put him right at peace, let me do my work without him fighting me one bit."

"Never heard another song like it," says Lance.

"Momma taught it to me," I say.

"She must have been one heck of a woman," says Lance.

"She was," I say. But then I think about Momma talking about cursing folks, about poisoning fields and turning wine to blood. "I mean, I think she was. I used to think she was the greatest woman in the world, the best and most prettiest.

But I'm not so sure anymore."

"No one's ever quite who you wish they were," says Chester.

"I just miss her a lot is all," I say.

I think I'm going to start crying again and I don't want to so I got to think of something else to say real fast.

"I love your house," I say.

Chester laughs. "Lance here built it himself, about two years back. We used to live in town."

"You lived in Templeton?" I say.

"Naw," says Lance, "we're from Moreberry, about thirty miles thataway. Still too close to Templeton for comfort though. What with that dadgum Preacher stirring everybody up. I like to know what durned religion he thinks it is he's preaching all the time, 'cause it sure ain't no gospel I ever heard."

When he mentions the Preacher I get real sad. We can't stay here, me and Tommy. Not if the Preacher's coming. It won't take long till he finds us. And who knows what he would do to Lance and Chester if he found out they helped us? He would kill them both. I wish Bobba could help us. I know she's out there in the woods somewhere, still speaking to me somehow in my noggin. But I guess our best hope is just to get Tommy to Aunt Barbara's as soon as possible, to make sure he's safe.

"Think Tommy will be able to walk soon?" I say. "At least

with a crutch or something? I could make him a crutch from a walking stick, if I had some rags."

Chester looks at me a little weird. "Honey dear, Tommy's not going to be able to walk for quite some time. A few days at least. He needs to lie flat, just where he is, else all that work I did will come undone real quick."

"But we got to go right now," I say.

"What's the hurry?" says Chester.

"You're worried about him hunting you, ain't you?" says Lance. "It's the Preacher, Chester. That Preacher's after them. Saw him when I was out hunting us some rabbits."

"The heck are they doing out here in the woods?" says Chester.

"That's why me and Tommy got to go, and got to go now," I say. "Because he's not gonna stop looking for us. Not me at least, and not ever."

"You knew the Preacher was after them, Lance?" says Chester. "You knew that and you brought them here anyway?"

"He can't push us around anymore," says Lance. "We moved once, out to the woods, to our own land. Ain't no law out here. He's got no authority over us."

"You should have told me," says Chester.

"I couldn't just leave a couple of kids out in the woods, could I?" says Lance. "The boy would be dead right now."

"Have you thought about what will happen to us if the

Preacher comes here?" says Chester. "What he will do to you and me?"

They're fighting because of me and Tommy. I feel awful about it. Everywhere we show up, something terrible happens. That's why we got to get out of here soon as we can.

"Hush, dangit," says Lance. He walks over to Chester and puts his arm around him. "You know good and well if that Preacher comes knocking, I'll be ready." He nods over to his rifle propped against the doorframe.

"And you think that will help us?" says Chester. Tommy hollers out in pain. "Lord. I'm going to get the boy some more water."

Chester walks outside. Lance sighs real loud.

"I'm sorry," I say. "I didn't mean to cause any trouble with y'all."

"Aw heck. Don't mind Chester. He'll come around," says Lance. "It just ain't been easy for us since the Preacher showed up. I got a feeling you know all about that."

Chester comes back in with a bucket of water. He sets it on the ground beside where Tommy's laid up.

"I'm sorry," he says to me.

"The Preacher scares me too," I say.

"Both y'all need to hush up with your worrying," says Lance. "I'll stand watch all night if I have to. Besides, who's a better shot than me? Name me one person in the whole dang county who can shoot half as good as ol' Lance?"

"No one," says Chester. He smiles a little. "Best shot I ever seen."

"We're getting mushy in front of the kiddos," says Lance.

"I don't mind," I say.

Tommy groans over on the table and I go and sit down by him. I put a new cold rag on his head. I sing a silent song for him to get better.

Chester sets to clearing the kitchen. Lance pulls a chair up by the window and sits, smoking, looking out, gun ready. All of the books they have, and I want to read them all. But there isn't any time. I have to be ready. Because the second Chester and Lance fall asleep is the second I bolt. There's no way the Preacher would do anything to Tommy with his leg all busted up, harmless and alone.

But if I'm here, people will get hurt, and bad. Because I know why the Preacher wants me dead now. I know so much more about him now, maybe more than anybody else in the whole world knows. I'm the key to what happened to him. I've seen what a hypocrite he really is. I've felt those words tangle themselves in the air, I know the way they can worm their way into a gentle mind. I know he's using magic to kill off anybody who disagrees with him, to cleanse the Hinterlands of anybody who doesn't fit in with his way of doing things. And if what he said in that memory's true, then I have magic in me too, and the Preacher'll never stop until I'm dead.

Somewhere far off there's a thunder grumble, a blink of lightning. The air smells sweet with rain. I know something big is coming, something that will change me and Tommy, change all of us forever. I know it's close as can be, just on the edge of the forest, ready to come like a tornado and blow us clean away.

The white kitty Princess Mona rubs up against my leg, a purring that tells my heart to stay. I scratch her behind the ears and she scrunches her face up. I'd love to stay here. I'd love to be Chester and Lance's daughter, to read books and cook and shoot guns for my whole forever, hidden out here in the woods cabin. But a storm is coming, and if I want to save anybody then I got to be gone before it gets here.

EIGHTEEN

The rain starts, a thousand tiny cat scratches on the roof. Lance sighs, leans back in his chair. Chester finishes tidying up and lies down on the bed, reading by candlelight. I ask if I can pick out a book to flip through and he says sure. I find a slim leather-bound thing, with no name and a drawing of a plant on it. The book is in a language I can't read, but it's full of pictures of strange flowers. Some are red and on fire. Some look like little blue eyeballs.

The nice thing about a book in a different language is that you can make it say whatever you want. The words are just pictures for your own words and all of a sudden the book is your book, it's your story that you're reading. That's how it is with all books, really, when you get down to it. This book is about a princess and her garden. All these plants are hers. Some of the plants are good, and some are less good. Some might even be evil. All of them are her friends though.

Tommy snores soft on the table. I walk over and kiss his cheek, muss his hair a little. He opens his eyes for a second and smiles at me. Chester's kept him woozy with herbs and tea, but not in a mean way like Bobba. I know his ankle hurts him so. I'm just glad he can sleep.

I'm sorry, Tommy. I whisper it right in his ear. *If I never get to tell you again. I'm sorry about your momma. I'm sorry about your leg. You're the only real friend I ever had.*

I crawl up on the table next to him and hold his hand and burrow myself into him like I seen a cub and bear do once. It's a safe feeling, warm and cozy. The roof, the fire, the books, Chester and Lance, Tommy. It's almost a family right here. It's almost what I've always wanted.

Too bad I can't let it last.

I wait and wait. The steady rain, Tommy's snoring. Chester sleeps with the book on his chest. Lance even seems like he's dozing a little in his chair, gun in his lap. His eyes are shut, and I can see his chest rise up with breath. He's as asleep as he'll get.

It's time. I ease myself off the table, just barely touch my bare feet to the floor.

"You wouldn't be thinking of running out on us now, would you?" says Lance.

He's still in the same sleep slump, just now he's got a big

eye cocked open and glaring right at me. It's his house, I don't feel like lying to him.

"How'd you know?"

"Figured," he says. "Heck, it's what I would do if I was you."

"So you gonna let me go?"

"Not on your life," he says, grinning.

I know it shouldn't, but it makes me smile too. It feels good to be wanted around, for someone to try and protect me.

"You know the Preacher will find me here," I say. "You know he'll hurt you and Chester. I don't want that on me. You been so good to me, haven't made me do anything, haven't asked anything of me. Didn't even poison me. Don't think I can thank you enough for all that."

"Well shoot, you don't have to get all sentimental about it," he says. "Anything happens to us, it ain't on you. This day's been coming for a long time. That Preacher was gonna show up here sooner or later, with a posse and a hanging rope. You know it as good as I do. Neither you nor God's got a thing to do with it. You just got him here a little faster is all."

"You gonna give us to him?"

"Naw," says Lance. "I don't know why he's hunting you, and I don't care to know. You're an innocent to me. Anything that happened to you ain't your fault at all. Now hush. I don't care what you got to say about it. It's tough for the likes of you two out there, kids on the run. Tough being out there in the world."

"Thanks, Lance." It's not enough, but it's all I got. "I mean it."

"This is my house. I built it," he says. "I ain't hurting no one, and I'm not going anywhere, no matter what that Preacher says." Lance pats his rifle. "Let him come. I can't wait."

The rain falls steady outside. The trees bend and bow and sway. Lightning cuts up the clouds and somehow above us I can still see the moon, just barely, like it's fighting to look down on us through the storm, like it's worried about us and wants to see.

The moon wins and she burns her light right through the storm clouds in a white beam that looks solid enough to climb on. The trees shake themselves like wet dogs and a fury of cardinals, hundreds maybe, fly through the rain and land in the trees until they are full of little fire tongues. The beam of moonlight dances and twirls until it's not moonlight anymore, it's a girl, it's me. All the birds peer down at me with crooked heads, they watch, but I don't notice, I dance and dance until I'm older, until I'm not a girl anymore, I'm my momma. Momma's in the long white dress she died in, but it isn't ripped, it isn't burned black and gone yet. She looks her eyes at me in the window.

"Momma," I say.

She has a book in her hand, the same book that I took from Bobba's tree, the one that mewls and caws like a baby. She clutches the book and walks toward me. But it's jerky and limping and as she walks farther from the moonlight she stumbles. The book is wailing, Momma thrusts it out to me, and I take it. It's warm in my hands and it cries until I stroke it, I sing softly to it. It curls up in my hands until it's a baby, until it's got gold-flecked eyes that look up in wonder, until the book is me.

The book is me and I can read every word. The symbols in the clouds, the scribbles in the bark, the holler of wolves out in the distance. All of it a new language that I can read with my bones, the blood from my heart, the tingling in my fingers. Every tiny thing is a word somebody's speaking, God singing the sunrise. This is how you do magic, I realize. You read the stories in everything, you speak the stories of the world.

Momma smiles at me. She smiles and smiles until she crumbles to dust.

The book screams and I drop it. I try to scoop Momma up, all the wind-scattered ashes of her, but the dust rises in the wind and my momma is in the air, I can't see a place where she isn't.

The cardinals in the trees cry out. They flap their wings and burst into flames, all of them a tiny fire each that becomes a big fire. The trees, the whole woods are burning. A family of deer burst from the tree line, their fur on fire. A white kitten out in the woods licks its burning paws.

"Goldeline," says a voice. I turn around and it's Tommy, fire in his hair, skin blistering, his clothes blackened and burning in front of me. He opens his mouth to scream and fire billows from his mouth. He's crying tears of flame and I look down and my own hands are fire, they're made of fire, and everything they touch burns.

I snap awake.

"I was dreaming," I say.

"Shhh," says Lance. "He's here."

NINETEEN

Through the window I see the Preacher, his long black coat, black wide-brimmed hat, standing alone in the rain and moonlight.

"He's been out there near an hour," says Lance. "Just standing there. Ain't said a word."

Chester's huddled up next to us.

"What's he doing?" says Chester.

"Not a clue," says Lance. "Waiting I guess."

"Waiting for what?" says Chester.

Lightning strikes and a big grin flashes across the Preacher's face. I know what he's waiting for.

He's waiting for me. He was waiting for me to wake up.

As if by magic he calls to me.

"Goldeline," says the Preacher. "Can you hear me, sweet

angel? Come out now, Goldeline."

The wind moans, the trees groan with the weight of the rain, bending low in the storm. The wind hurts the trees. Chester blows out the candle. In the house it becomes all dark, the fire just embers, the lightning tossing its whiteness through the window in flashes.

"Come on out, Goldeline. It's time for you to be healed, darling. Don't you want to be free of all this running, all this wickedness and sin? Don't you want to be cleansed? Like the Book says, 'To the creature who longs for the fire, so shall the fire be granted to it, and it shall be made clean.'"

The Preacher's voice is so lovely, full of scrape and holler like the low notes of a fiddle, rich as the saddest songs.

"That ain't all the Book says," says Lance.

The Preacher walks toward the house. A gun blast rings powerful in my ears. Lance fired at him through the open window. The shot kicks up mud on the Preacher's shoes.

"Now I wouldn't take one step closer, Preacher, if I was you," hollers Lance. "This is my land. You got no authority here."

"The earth is God's, and everything in it," says the Preacher.

"Yeah, but you ain't God," says Lance. "Lest you forgot."

The Preacher claps his hands.

"Isaac Lancelot Jeffries, that must be you!"

Lance shakes his head.

"Good Lord," he says, "how does he remember my full name? How'd he know it in the first place?"

Because there's power in a name, but I don't say it.

"Who wants to know?" hollers Lance.

"Oh, you know good and well who I am." The Preacher grins. "And you know why I'm here."

"And if you know anything else about me other than my name," says Lance, "then you know I ain't gonna give them to you."

"I was hoping you'd say that," says the Preacher. "I'm assuming you have your fairer half in there with you." He cups his hands to his mouth. "Chesterfield Leonides Paul, you in there?" he yells. "Your mother is ashamed of you. Ninety-three years old, still weeps for you daily, sick in your sin, judgment yipping at your heels like an old mutt."

I turn to Chester and he's crying. The lightning makes crystals of his tears. Lance puts a hand on Chester's shoulder, touches his face, wipes the tears off his cheek. The closeness they have is theirs and they can't share it, not with me. But it feels so good, so real to see it, love in all the sick dark of the night.

"We have blasphemers in our midst." The Preacher looks around the house, beyond it, to the woods, like there's a whole mass of people I can't see, like he's preaching to the trees. "Sinners, given over to a reprobate mind. Oh, they shall receive the full recompense of their error."

The Preacher shouts into the darkness, waving his hands while the lightning flashes like he's controlling it, like a dark magician of the skies hollering out to a ghost congregation.

"Filthy dreamers they are, defilers of the flesh, the despised of kings, speaking untruth. Clouds without water, blown about by strange winds. Poisoned trees, without fruit, nothing but chaff for the fire. Wandering stars, for whom is reserved the blackest darkness forever."

I know that bit. The Preacher's quoting from the Book, one of the strangest passages, and also one of the loveliest. Too bad it's about sinners and all the bad stuff that's going to happen to them. It's so pretty it should be about the heroes, the good ones that God is glad to have in his heaven. It doesn't make sense that some of the prettiest parts of the Book are all about evil.

Little eyes of fire shine in the dark. What are those? Glints of metal.

"Why don't you wake up young Thomas, Goldeline," says the Preacher. "All he done is on you, you know that, right? You know his sins against the Lord are your very own. His act of theft and violence. That's yours, Goldeline."

The Preacher is right. He's always right. That's the thing about the Preacher. He knows and he accuses. He's got his claws deep in me, like he's trying to yank some wounded bit of me out.

"It's not your fault, Goldy," says Tommy. I didn't know

he was awake. He shakes his head at me. "I don't feel very good."

I walk over to the table and help him up. He leans on my shoulder, and together we can kind of walk like that. We hobble back to Lance and Chester, all four of us by the window huddled together like a sad battered family. I'm scared, and I don't want to die, I don't want any of us to die. But it feels so good to stand with other people, to not be alone. For so long it's just been one little girl against the dark and now it's the four of us.

"You can escape your damnation, young Thomas," says the Preacher. "You can come out here and I will forgive you, wipe your sins clean. God will do that for you, if you just come out here and be with me."

"You can go if you want, Tommy," I say. "I won't be mad."

"Heck no," says Tommy. "Besides, it isn't God I'm scared of." He points at the window. "It's him."

"Come on out, little one. Come on out to me."

"Forget it," says Tommy. "I ain't coming."

"Hellfire it is!" roars the Preacher. He seems taller now, fiercer, his shadow against the moonlight stretches all the way to the front door, large as a dragon.

Torches. Hellfire. My dream.

"Lance!" I scream. "He's gonna burn the house down!"

But I can already smell it, the roof lit up, the smoke.

"How?" says Lance.

"There's men in the woods," I say. "Lots of them. They're everywhere."

Lance flings open the door. A rush of cool wind and rain swarms in like an angry ghost.

"I built this house," he says. "I built it with my own hands."

He steps outside the door and part of the frame is shot off. Lance grabs his hand. He falls back inside the house and I shut the door after him.

The Preacher cackles.

"You're surrounded! You got a whole heavenly host around you and they are armed with rifles! You step one foot out of that door and we shoot you. You stay in there and you burn. Those are your two options, but the Evil One gets you either way."

I hear it before I can feel it, the crackling of the fire, the way the wood and straw are swallowed, taken in, and become fire itself. Soon it licks the inside of the roof, shows itself orange and starving, sparks scattering wild as ants across the ceiling, to the curtains, the fire hungry to grasp everything, to take it all into itself. Chester wraps Lance's hand in a rag. There's nothing I can do to help. I just watch the fire spread, knowing I brought this smoke and doom on us all.

Cinders fall like snow. The books catch, all the words I'll never read gone up in smoke like prayers, the whole house like a torch to signal God with. The smoke is so thick, so horrible, like the black storm clouds swooped down from the sky and came in through the window, spitting fire, pouring themselves down our throats. We have to crouch low to get under it. Chester and Lance carry Tommy between them, they try to keep him safe from the flames, from the heat and the burning. A piece of the roof crumbles and falls, embers scattering bright as jewels across the floor. The fire surrounds us, the beams of the house seem to bend down, to dip the flames closer to us. Smoke burns my eyes, it burns my throat. And everywhere is heat, is bright, is fire.

"Goldeline," says Lance. "You get your cloak, the one I found you in. Bundle up good in it."

The cloak isn't far from me, the fire hasn't touched it yet. I crawl on all fours to under the table where I stashed it. I put it on, wrap up tight in it even though it's so hot in here.

"Me and Chester are going to carry Tommy out," he says. "When we get to the door you take off around back and head for the woods. They'll be distracted by us. No way the Preacher will shoot Tommy, wounded as he is."

"But what about you two?" I say.

"We haven't got any other choice," says Chester. He kisses me on the forehead. "We're ready. At least you'll make it."

"Don't leave me," says Tommy. He grabs at my hand but I pull it away.

Lance and Chester hoist Tommy's arms and legs up between them.

"Open the door and let us out," says Lance. "Then you run for the woods."

"Don't leave me!" screams Tommy.

I can't even look at him. I stay low and pull the door open. When no gunshots fire, Chester and Lance and Tommy run for it. I run too, but the other way, around the house, crouched low, in my smoke-colored cloak. The Preacher's men are gathered in front of the house, some on horses, some with rifles, some with torches, their faces lit red by the fire. But they aren't looking at me. They're all focused on Chester and Lance and Tommy. One man raises his rifle, a sick smile on his face. I run for the darkness of the forest, the freedom of the trees, the dirt-worn bandit roads. If I run and keep running I can stay ahead of the Preacher, I can be free of him, free of the fire and the burning and the death, death, death trailing me like a hellhound that's got my sniff, that howls low and cold in my heart.

But can I really leave Chester and Lance and Tommy behind? Can I trust the Preacher to be merciful to them, even though they helped me? Is mercy a word he even knows?

I got to make a decision now. I could keep running. I could follow this road forever, I could outrun the Preacher until one of us finally trips up and dies. I could leave a trail of dead people who loved me, who took care of me, bring fire and doom on anyone who was nice enough to give me so much as a cup of water when I was thirsty.

The rain has stopped, the trees glisten in the starlight. The smell of smoke in the darkness, the chipped-bone moon above. Out in the woods an owl makes its music and I can hear it, only I can understand it. Behind me scurries Chester and Lance's kitten, Princess Mona. She purrs up next to my leg, a warm thing in the horrible burning night. I pick her up and she meows at me, and there's no doubting what that means.

I understand now. I understand everything so clearly. I touch my hand out on the bark of a tree and I can read it same as it was language. The moonlight sings down on me. The whole world is a warm animal holler blooming out in the deep dark, a beautiful thing, filled with critters and angels and people, the earth a great music maker with a heart of fire. I know now, and I understand.

Ever since Momma died, I've been looking for a home, some place where I belonged, where I was safe and happy and everybody loved me. Well, maybe that kind of a home just isn't in the cards for me yet. Maybe the only home I got right now is in myself. I'm Goldeline. No one can take that away from me. Not the Preacher, not anybody else.

I don't want to run anymore. I don't want anyone else dying on account of me. I hold Princess Mona close to me, a good weapon against the darkness. I walk back toward the fire, toward the burning house, toward him. Toward the Preacher.

Men in black cloaks have all gone down and circled Lance and Chester and Tommy. Two stand by the Preacher. I recognize them. It's Regis, and the third man from the fire. They both got guns at the ready.

"It ain't too late for you," says the Preacher. "All you have to do is repent. That's it."

But Chester clutches Lance, holds on to him like he's the only steady thing in the world, like he's the tall tree in a windstorm, the one that won't topple. But I can see it from here, the way his head droops, Lance is hurt. Blood dribbles from his mouth and he looks terrified.

I'm past the burning house now, creeping quiet as I can. No one's noticed me yet. I can see Tommy down by everyone's boots, laid out and crying.

Regis aims the rifle at Chester and Lance.

I can't let them die. I can't have their ghosts follow me too. I got too many ghosts, too many dead ones that haunt my dreams. The world seems small as the three people encircled by guns and fire, huddled together in fear.

"Stop!" I scream in my best Gruff voice, my hair let loose, wild and white, all the mean and tough I got brought up to my face. In my arms Princess Mona hisses and claws. The men lower their guns and make room for me in the circle. I stand right in the center, in front of Chester and Lance, in front of Tommy. I stand, fully scowled, a wicked cat in my arms, a bandit, a witch, just like my momma.

The Preacher cackles wild.

"Goldeline, the little girl lost, she has returned!"

"You can't shoot them," I say. "I won't let you."

The Preacher crouches down to look me in the eyes. I flinch at his breath, the rotten sulfur stink of it.

"Little one," he says, "you will find I can do anything I please."

"I know why you murdered my momma," I say. The rain begins to fall again, and steam rises from the ground, the crackle and sizzle of rain on fire. "I was there in the window. You know. You saw me. That's why you been hunting me. That's why you been trying to kill me."

"I don't want to kill you, Goldeline," the Preacher says, "I want to save you."

"Save me?" I say.

I don't understand.

"Don't you know?" says the Preacher. "That's why I've kept you alive so long. You must repent, Goldeline. Because your mother was a *witch*." He says the word nasty, stabs it in me like a twisted dagger. "And you got the same witch's blood in you. The same devil's heart. A witch, you are. A sorceress. You deserve to burn, same as your mother.

"But that is not God's plan for you, Goldeline. He wants you to be cleansed, and so do I. God wants to cleanse you of your mother. He wants to wash you clean of her sin, her witchcraft. God wants to save you from your mother."

The kitten struggles in my arms. The Preacher's words swirl around me like bats.

"Because all this pain is your mother's fault. The people you robbed, that little boy's hurt leg, your dead bandit friend. They all died because of your mother. She is the cause of all this misery. She was a wicked woman, a temptress, evil to her heart's core. But it isn't too late for you, Goldeline. I've come to forgive you. I'll even take you in as my daughter. My own little girl. You'll have a home, a family, everything you ever wanted."

The Preacher leans in close to me, whispering, his breath hot on my ear. *You remember how I used to be. How I would read the Book to you when you were a child, how I took care of you and your mother. We were happy, Goldeline. It could be like that again. I want to be good to you, like a daddy would. Like I offered to your mother all those years ago.*

I am shaking, and the kitten shivers in my arms. The Preacher pulls his face away from mine. He speaks louder now, so everyone can hear him.

"All you have to do is repent, Goldeline. Renounce your mother. Call her what she was: a witch, a servant of the Evil One. Confess it with your mouth. I'll forgive you, God will forgive you. All you have to do is come with me, be my family, and you'll be free of your mother forever."

The Preacher reaches his hand out to me and brushes the ashes from my cheek. His fingers are soft, not at all like

Gruff's. His eyes blue and sparkling, almost pleading.

The kitten hisses and thunder cracks above me. I remember again, Momma talking with the Preacher like they were old friends. I remember the Preacher attacking her. I remember every awful truth of it. I remember his name.

"Mr. Cyrus," I say. "Cyrus Cantor."

I did it. I said his name out loud. I named him. Above me flits a cardinal, a red bird like a tongue of fire over my head.

"Cyrus Cantor," I say again, louder, more unscared. Because there's power in a name, magic in who a person truly is.

More cardinals now, two, three, six. They perch in the trees, gathering like judges. The cardinals are listening.

"Cyrus Cantor," I say a third time, because magic comes in threes.

A single cardinal lands on my shoulder. The kitten doesn't even flinch at it.

"Yes, Goldeline?" says the Preacher. His eyes are wide, begging me to forgive him.

"You're a fraud, Cyrus Cantor," I say. "You're a faker and a liar, and I'm not scared of you anymore."

For just a second his eyes wince with pain, like what I said hurt him, and I realize he really did want me to come home with him. He really did want to be my family. But it only lasts a second.

"Do you reject the salvation of the Lord?" says Cyrus, in full booming preacher voice again.

"It ain't salvation if it means I have to belong to you," I say.

Cyrus stands to his full height. His nightmare-black suit, his wild white hair. He gestures wide to the circle of men surrounding us.

"You have heard it yourselves! Before a crowd of witnesses she has denied the Lord. She is her mother's daughter, corrupted through her bones, deep into her soul. God's mercy is useless on her. She stands condemned."

He looks over to Regis, whose gun is trained at me.

"Shoot her," says Cyrus.

I watch Regis's hands shake, his confused look back to the Preacher and then to the people of the town. Because that's who they are—I recognize so many of them now in the torchlight. They are from Templeton, the Townies, the same ones who condemned my momma. Mr. Busby, the baker who used to give me sweets, Mr. Smithee, who owned all the pigs. I know these men. I used to. They were there when Momma died. They remember.

All around us more and more cardinals gather in the unburned trees, the full of them bright as autumn, a forest of movable fire. I can feel a change, something quiet and hidden rising up in the invisibles of me, like something broke open inside of me, filling my heart with fire and with light. I stand taller now, I speak louder in a voice I've heard a million times, a voice that isn't mine but has been with me all along.

"You wanted my momma for your own, Cyrus Cantor," I say. "You came by our house and begged her."

"I begged for nothing," says Cyrus. "Shoot her."

Regis looks back and forth between me and Cyrus. He glances over his shoulder at some of the other men. They open their eyes wide at him, maybe confused, like maybe they don't know who to trust right now.

"I can't just shoot her," says Regis. "She's a little girl."

The kitten meows in my arms.

"You loved my momma," I say. "You brought her flowers at night. You wanted to marry her."

Mr. Busby takes his hat off, looks down at his feet. He's remembering. He's remembering how pretty Momma was, how maybe some time in his life he wanted to bring her flowers too. I can feel it, I don't know how, but I know it in my heart.

"What's this about, Preacher?" says the third man.

They're questioning him now. They won't do just anything he says. Something is changing, in the sky, in the clouds and in the wind. I can feel a moon rising in my blood. The Townies are waking up.

"Lies," hisses Cyrus. "Did I not warn you all? Did I not tell you she had a serpent's tongue? This girl speaks with the very words of the Evil One, with the authority of the grave. They are sweet to your ears but sour in your belly. Is a large fire not set by a tiny spark? Her words are the spark to a furnace full of lies. Shoot her now lest that fire consume you too."

"You begged her to marry you. You tried to force her," I say. "I saw it. But she fought you. She fought hard, my momma did. That's how you got your scar right there, ain't it?" I'm crying now. This is all I got. "Tell them, Cyrus Cantor, you murderer. Tell them what you did to my momma."

I point at the Townies, and two or three of them take a step backward, as if I'm accusing them too. One shorter man, I think he was a butcher in Templeton, he meets my eyes for a second. His are gray as a stone, and he drops his head down, like he's ashamed.

"You can't murder a witch," says Cyrus. "You can only give her what she deserves."

He spins around, his arms out wide, his body making a tall black cross.

"I spent five years doing penance," he howls. "Five years wandering in the desert. Five years of pain and suffering. Then I saw it. A vision. I saw your mother, Goldeline. I saw her as a snake with red eyes and fangs, gliding across the waters. I saw a white worm cross the sky above me and the earth tremble. I was given a mission. I was to rid the world of all the magic types, of the sinners and gamblers and outlaws, of anyone who didn't fit in this world. To make a new world, to cleanse it. And I was given the power to do it. See, it wasn't my fault what happened, what I did. I'm blameless. It was your mother's." He points his finger at my face. "Same as you."

"I heard about enough of this junk," says the third man. He points his own rifle at Cyrus. No one stops him. The men back away from Cyrus. They don't want to be near him. It's like he's cursed, like he's infected with some looming disease. His power is waning. They don't want what's coming for him to get them too.

I can feel the magic rise up in me, covering me like a white dress, like my skin is made of moonlight. I can feel myself glow. I take a step toward Cyrus. I am growing taller in his eyes, I can feel it. I am growing more lovely and more beautiful. The light from inside me is borne all over my body, it's shining from the gold in my eyes. I can control it. My light is mightier than Cyrus's darkness ever can be. I can make Cyrus see what I want him to see.

I smile at Cyrus and his eyes go wide.

Because Cyrus isn't seeing me anymore. He's seeing someone else. All he sees now is Momma.

"I loved you," says Cyrus.

The men gape openmouthed. The trees bow to me in the wind. Cardinals rise over our heads in whirls of fire.

"Oh God," says Cyrus. "What did I do?"

Cyrus falls backward, stumbling. I walk toward him, slow and brave, elegant, graceful, the way Momma walked. My head held high, my back straight, my hair billowing like a snowstorm behind me. He won't let me near him, he staggers backward with every step I take toward him, he's afraid of me. I know my eyes spark gold brighter than fire, brighter than Chester and Lance's home engulfed in flames, the doorway sagging, the pit of fire Cyrus is backing himself toward.

I'm my own. That's my magic. Momma named me. I'm Goldeline, and I can do what she couldn't.

"Stay away from me," says Cyrus, stumbling backward, his hands covering his face. "Don't come any closer."

I don't stop, I keep on walking, sure now, steady and brave. Cyrus is nearly to the burning house, he has his back right up to it. He must feel the heat lap at him, the flames longing to swallow him whole.

I take a final step toward him. The men watch in awe as Cyrus turns to run away from me, as he flings himself right into the burning house. The roof caves in, embers scattering wild as birds into the black night. The house crumbles and falls. Cyrus vanishes into the flame and crash and smoke.

The cardinals swoop together in a great cloud of red and vanish into the night.

He's dead. The Preacher is dead. The shadow that stretched over my whole life is vanished. All this running, all this death. It's over. I don't know why but I'm sad somehow, like I lost something forever.

There's a quiet over all Cyrus's men, the Townies. Cyrus's spell has been broken. All the men blink awake, their minds unpoisoned for the first time in months, maybe even years. They look down at their boots, at the sky, anywhere but at me. They're ashamed, of what they've done, of what they almost did. Tommy's shivering on his stomach, eyes bleary, not even crying anymore.

"Somebody help me," I say. "He's sick. We got to get him to the doctor."

"What just happened?" says the third man. "I don't understand."

"This boy is dying. His name is Tommy and he's my friend. You have to help him."

The third man sighs.

"We got us a wounded kid here," he says to the men, "sick cold in the rain. We got to get him back to town, to Dr. Gilbert."

He and a few others pick Tommy up and sit him on a horse with another man.

"I'm coming too," I say. "I'm not leaving Tommy."

The man looks at me for a minute, then nods. I climb up with them, holding Tommy close to me, keep him sitting up, ready to ride back into town. Before we leave I see Regis walk up to Chester and Lance. He bows his head a little in front of them, as if he's paying penance.

"I'm sorry about your house," he says.

Lance looks up at him, red-eyed and bleeding. He doesn't say anything. But something happens, quiet as a sunrise. Maybe an understanding, or what might be. But I don't get to see what happens next, because we're riding, riding fast, down the road and back toward Templeton.

TWENTY

t takes hours and hours of riding. I think so at least. It's hard to tell, I'm so tired. But I hold on tight to Tommy and though he cries sometimes from the pain he never falls off, he never even totters. When we get to Templeton it's almost morning. The streets are just waking up, some people already going about their Townie business. The strange thing is how I don't hate them anymore. I don't forgive them, mind you. I don't know if I can ever do that. But I don't hate them either. They don't look evil or scary to me. An old man with a lump on his head pops his knuckles. A pigtailed little girl carries a loaf of bread to her momma. They just look, well, normal, just folks out in the morning, like anybody else. It's strange to me how little the town has changed but how different I feel about it, like maybe I'm the one who changed.

The third man rides us straight to the jail.

"Don't get the wrong idea," he says. "It's just the safest place for y'all, till we can get everything sorted. I'll off and fetch the doctor."

It's the first time I've ever seen the real inside of a jail. It looks about like I thought it would, one cell, iron bars, and a little cot. There aren't any prisoners, which is all right with me. The third man lays Tommy down on the cot, helping him prop his leg up so it doesn't hurt. Hanging on one of the walls is a wanted poster, one of me and Tommy, our faces in black ink with *WANTED* printed in huge letters up top. I don't know, it makes me feel good seeing it. I can't explain why. Maybe something left over of Gruff in me, something that is a little proud to be on a poster, to have folks out searching for me. To be a wanted woman, a real bandit. If I didn't think they'd get mad I would roll it up and keep it for myself.

"I've never been in a real jail before," says Tommy.

"Me either," I say.

"I don't like it," he says.

"Can't say it's my favorite."

"Goldeline?"

"Yeah, Tommy?"

"Our adventure's over, isn't it?"

Adventure? I never thought of it like that. I always just thought it was life.

"I guess so," I say.

"Thank the Lord," says Tommy.

We're not in the jail ten minutes before the doctor comes calling. He's bald, with a white mustache, spectacles on his nose, bumbling around like he just woke up. He sets about examining Tommy's leg. He's followed by a fat lady in a fancy purple dress, long and frilly with ruffles. The dress is so tight I don't know how she crammed her body into it. There's some danger to her, like her dress could explode and spill her naked butt out at any moment.

"Where is he?" says the woman. "Where is my darling Thomas?"

I've been at Aunt Barbara's a year now. It was fine, all good times, at first. For starters, Aunt Barbara is the richest person I ever met. Her house has two stories, built just for her, if you can believe it. I even had my own bed, my own room. First week home she took me shopping, bought me all kinds of dresses, all colors, perfume, my own bone-handled mirror. She taught me how to put on makeup, which I did until Tommy saw me one day and laughed himself silly.

"You look like a clown," he said. "You look like you could be in the circus."

I would have clobbered him, except that's not how it worked with Aunt Barbara. In fact, you couldn't hardly do anything at Aunt Barbara's house. She wouldn't tolerate any noise, not while she was reading, or had ladies over, or even when she was just sitting there, not doing a thing. You had to sit quiet, in shoes that pinched your feet. And the dinner parties, the tea parties. Never say a word, hold your back straight, chin up, keep quiet, like I was some durn porcelain doll.

Don't scowl, Goldeline. You have such a pretty face when you smile with it.

Don't sigh.

Don't droop your head, it's rude.

Don't interrupt.

Don't.

Don't.

Don't.

It's all I ever hear.

Tommy wasn't much help either, at least not at first. When we got to Carrolton, he went around telling everybody I was his girlfriend. It was hard to put a stop to that. I was scared of hurting his feelings. But once he got it through his skull that I wasn't anybody's girlfriend, we were fine. Best friends even, like I never had before. Aunt Barbara has an upright piano, her very own, and she always let Tommy play whenever he felt like it. It was good to have a house full of music.

Winter was lovely, with a big fire in the hearth and all these blankets and warm clothes and never being cold.

Especially when Aunt Barbara was at one of her million social engagements and it was just me and Tommy in the house. Aunt Barbara tried taking me to some of her events and dinners and things, but I failed her so bad at all of them that she finally just let me alone. That was much better, when she left me and Tommy sitting by the fire. That's when it felt most like family. I'd read to him from an old fairy book, or sometimes I'd just make up a story of my own. Those were the best times, the happiest I'd had since Momma died.

Still, I didn't like the other kids much, all Tommy's friends. Because he made friends real fast, even though he's still got a little bit of a limp. People always wanted to be his friend because of all the stories. Our stories, his and mine. He'd tell them to any kid who would listen, rattle off about him and me being bandits, me being the legendary "Ghost Girl of the Woods." I liked that part, all the other girls, dainty soft little darlings who I could whoop with my pinky finger, looking at me with big terrified eyes. I liked parading around them in my fancy dresses, bossing them, knowing I was prettier and smarter and tougher than they'd ever be.

"You got to stop it," Tommy said to me one day. "Being so mean to them. How do you ever expect to make any friends if everybody's scared of you all the time?"

"I don't want any other friends," I said. "You're my friend. That's the only friends I need. Why do I have to have any other friends?"

He sighed and hopped away, with his limping broke-legged step.

I started spending more and more time alone, at the edge of Carrolton. My favorite spot was right outside the city, near a fringe of old buildings and a short stone wall about waist high, just before the town vanished into woods. It was as close as I could get to somewhere I loved and still be in the town. Nearby was an abandoned church, the congregation long driven out or died, with an old graveyard sitting right next to it. Only twenty or thirty busted and unkempt headstones were left, and the church building was roofless except for the spire, a crooked finger pointing up to heaven. It was maybe my favorite place in all Carrolton. I would go there and hide on my own sometimes, just to be secret.

On those days I would lean against a headstone and watch the sun crawl across the sky, the shadows of the tree limbs stretch into bony fingers and gray out into the dusk light. Sometimes the tree shadows on the grass were like words in a book, and sometimes I thought I could read them, like the trees were spelling out stories with their hands. It was like everything was talking to me. The leaves would swirl and I could catch a glimpse of something, a picture and a word. Caterpillars thick as baby arms traced their names on tombstones. I would sit and watch the spiders build homes in the air, strands of string wispy as breath, like the spiders were speaking out their world. The spiders would catch bigger bugs in the webs, hung up on spider words, and spin their dinner up tight, wrapped like a present. I would listen to the animal sounds windblown from the forest, the strange scratching song of the woods while a cold breeze prickled my neck.

Sometimes it felt like the woods knew me, that as I lay dozing the wind would whisper my name and I'd jolt awake, startled, Bobba's voice still ringing in my ears, the faint smell of baking wafting through the air. On those days I hated the kids in town most of all. Tommy would bring a kid over to play and I'd rather spit than speak his name.

Even so, life with Tommy and Aunt Barbara was fine, more or less. But then I did something. At least, I think I did, and it made everything go wrong.

A month ago, Tommy asked me to go play hide-and-seek with some of the other kids, a few boys, and this one horrible girl, a pigtailed, gappy-toothed blabby rich girl named Sylvia.

"Ugh," I said, "why?"

"Because she's great!" Tommy said. "When you get to know her, you'll just love her."

That's when I realized Tommy had a crush on Sylvia. What was even worse was that he expected me to become friends with her. But I said I would go, and I promised to be nice.

We played on the edge of Carrolton, by my happy

graveyard place. Playing there was my idea. I figured if I had to be with the other kids, at least it could happen somewhere I liked.

Sylvia counted at base, the giant oak tree that marked the beginning of the woods. I didn't much want to play, so after everyone ran away to hide, I snuck off into the woods, even though it was off-limits. I missed the woods so much I couldn't help it. Besides, Sylvia had only counted to sixteen. She still had thirty-four more to go. I crept past her and into the trees, just a few hundred feet, not far at all. I nestled behind a sprung-out root of a big leaning oak. I figured I could sit awhile and let Sylvia run down someone else before I snuck back and took my usual hiding spot behind an old cracked tombstone that just said *Stump* on it.

It was nice and cozy in my spot. I took off the shoes Aunt Barbara made me wear and let the dirt touch my toes. A bird sung out, a robin. They always sound so sad to me. It was the loveliest sound I'd heard in months, a mystery voice, not at all human, calling from where I couldn't see. I decided this was my new favorite spot, and I would come here any time I wanted, even if it was in the woods and off-limits. This was a safe spot. I shut my eyes and listened and smiled, let all the forest smells and sounds and feels swallow me up.

"I caught you!" chirped an awful girl voice. I opened my eyes. Sylvia stood there, her ugly finger poking out at me. "I caught you and that means you're it!"

"How did you know I was out here?" I said.

"I saw you when I was counting," she said. "I peeked."

"You cheated," I said.

"Well, you cheated first," said Sylvia. "The woods is off-limits. Everybody knows that." She was so pleased with herself it made me want to sock her. "Doesn't matter anyway. You're still it."

Sylvia skipped off through the trees, toward the town wall, singing, "Goldy's it, Goldy's it, I caught Goldeline!"

I got mad. It was her voice I think, the shrill horribleness of it. It made me crazy, like when rusty metal is scraped together. I shut my eyes and plugged my ears and tried to block it out. But in my mind I still saw Sylvia, plain as day, skipping toward town. I saw all the darkness of the woods stirring, black and alive. I twitched my fingers, gathering it all together, all the dusky damp places, the tree shadows, the cool spots under rocks—I gathered the dark together into something I could hold, twisted and gnarled as an old oak branch, cold and heavy in my hands. I swung it at Sylvia, straight at her knee. It was all in my head that I did this, like a make-believe game I was playing alone with myself.

I opened my eyes when I heard the crack, like a tree branch breaking from frost. Sylvia's leg snapped to the side, right in half, at the knee. She screamed and fell into the dirt. Sylvia rolled over and lifted her leg and when she did the bottom part, shin and ankle and foot, flopped over wrong.

Sylvia screamed and screamed. All the kids came running up.

"What happened?" said a kid named Wallace. He lived up the street from me and Tommy. I liked him okay.

"She tripped," I said.

"You tripped her," said Wallace. "I know you did."

"How could I have tripped her from all the way back here?" I said.

Tommy ran up and stopped, staring at me all weird.

"What's wrong?" I said.

"Look," he said, and pointed behind me.

A cardinal perched like a rose on a bare branch, eye level with me. I hadn't seen one in so long. It cocked its head to the side, gazing up at me, eyes black and questioning, like it was listening to me, waiting for my command. When I didn't move it darted off into the woods, just a normal bird. But its eyes had scared me. Like the cardinal had expected something from me.

And there was Tommy, staring at me too. Tommy knew. He walked over to Sylvia and held her hand until the doctor came. She cried all over him.

Tommy stopped asking me to play after that. It was fine, if lonely. I didn't like those other kids anyway.

When Aunt Barbara said that me and Tommy would start school in the fall, I told her that I didn't want to go.

"But, Goldeline, darling, you'll do so well in school," she

said. "You're so very smart. I've hired Mrs. Jessup from the parish to come and instruct you. She'll help you catch up to all the other kids."

"I don't need any catching up," I said.

"That is for me to decide," said Aunt Barbara. "Oh, don't make such a face. It isn't like I'm the devil now. Haven't I been good to you?"

"Yes, ma'am," I said. "You've been very good to me. But . . ."

"That's the spirit," she said. "We'll make a lady out of you yet."

I just sat and stared at a spear of sunlight come through the window. All the dust dangled and floated in it, glowing like magic. Funny how light can do that, make crummy old dust glow. It made me miss the woods, the trees, where light did all kinds of amazing things that it never got to do in a city.

It only took me a week to hate Mrs. Jessup. She just wants to teach me Book stuff, and not even the Book stuff I like. She wants me to learn the sacred catechisms, the holy creeds, which of the seven candles get lit during worship and in what order, all that ceremonial junk. I try to ask her about the story about the witch who gave the sad king bread, or the time God's big finger wrote mysteries on the banquet hall wall, but she won't have any of it. Nope, all Mrs. Jessup wants to talk about are rules and rules and more rules. But what about the stories?

No one here will ever let me alone. What's worse, when someone finally does—like Tommy, my only true friend in the world—I miss him. I don't understand anything about myself, how I feel. I don't understand what happened in the woods with Sylvia, same as what happened with the Preacher, except darker, meaner. I know I did something, and it was magic. I just don't know how.

But I want to know. I want to learn. About Momma, about magic, about where I come from. I know Bobba's out there, somewhere. I know she's got some answers for me, if I can only find her. Something tells me I will. Something tells me Bobba knows I'm coming for her, that she's getting impatient already, waiting.

I started stealing things, small stuff, like apples and teaspoons and even a butter knife once, just to do it. I keep them all in a secret spot, under a loose board in my closet. I know it's wicked of me, but it makes me feel better, like I'm not totally stuck, like I have a little bit of power in the city world.

I miss the woods. I miss campfires and waking up at dawn, covered in dew. I miss hearing owls at night, wandering wild and alone, nothing but bandits for friends. I miss the music and the wine. I miss the whole forest singing to me, telling me its secrets. Mostly though I miss Gruff. I miss him every day.

That's why I'm leaving tonight. Aunt Barbara's off at a gala somewhere, and there's nobody to look after me but a maid and she's long asleep. I think Aunt Barbara will be glad to be quit of me. I think I'm doing her a favor.

Tommy is different, though. He hasn't hardly spoken to me since what happened to Sylvia. We're barely even friends anymore, not like we used to be. But I can't just leave him without a good-bye. After he goes to bed, I sneak up to his room and creak open the door. He's asleep already, and he doesn't stir. I pull the covers back and crawl into bed with him.

"You're leaving?" he says.

"I thought you were sleeping," I say.

"Is it because of Sylvia?"

"I didn't mean to hurt her."

"Yes, you did."

"Yeah, I guess I did. I just didn't know it would do anything," I say. "I'm sorry, Tommy."

"I love you," he says.

I pull him close to me and we hold each other, same as we did those nights in the forest, clinging together like the broke-hearted orphans we are. No one else could understand what it's like between me and Tommy, what we went through, like we'll forever have a secret that's just ours, that we can always come back to, that will always draw us back together. I hope so, at least. When Tommy's breathing slows and he fidgets his feet a little under the covers, I know he's actually asleep. But as I slide out from under the covers, Tommy, still sleeping, grabs hold of my foot and kisses it once softly. My heart clenches in my chest. I don't know. It almost makes me want to stay. But I pull myself free, fix the blanket around him, tucking him in like I know he likes. I shut the door quiet behind me and try not to ruin it all by crying.

In my room I pack a light bag, just a spare dress, a jug of water, some bread, my favorite fairy book. I put on Zeb's momma's cloak, smoke-colored and easy to miss. I guess it's mine now, as much as anything is. It's still dark night out, the moon a gray smudge under the clouds. Rain sizzles on the roof, just enough sound to cover my footsteps down the stairs, the door creaking shut. Outside I feel free already. The streets are empty, there's no one to catch me.

I open my mouth and taste the wild free drops of the rain. They splash on my nose and I laugh and hum one of Momma's songs, the nothingsong, just me and the owls and bats and all the hidden creatures in the night. I know there's a road outside of town, and past that some woods, dark and lovely, and I don't know but maybe there is a light for me to follow, a candle stuck in a window somewhere, calling me home.

ACKNOWLEDGMENTS

Thanks to Mary Marge Locker, genius and love of my heart. Thanks to Mom and Dad and Chris, the best family a guy could ask for. Gigantic thanks to Jess Regel, the greatest ever, without whom none of this would be possible. From the bottom of my heart, Jess, I cannot thank you enough. Thanks to Andrew Eliopulos for the keen eye and brilliant editorial work. This book wouldn't be what it is without your kindness, patience, and heart. Thanks to Matt Wise for the earliest faith, for being the first person to give me a shot. Thanks to Matt Saunders for the most amazing cover of all time. Thanks to Megan Abbott, for the friendship and guidance and more than I can even begin to list right now. Thanks to William Boyle, the best dude in the entire world.

Thanks to Jack Pendarvis, forever and always my friend and hero. Thanks to Liam Baranauskas, the wise and brave. Thanks to McKay McFadden, E. M. Tran, Brendan Steffan, and the esteemed members of the Good Idea Club. I didn't know there were people like you guys in the world, and I'll never stop being grateful. Thanks to P. S. Dean, brother of my soul, as well as all the Heroes of 804. Thanks to Len Clark always, my first-ever creative partner. Thanks to Michael Bible for opening this door wide for me, and for loving books just the same way I do. Seriously, Michael, I really, really appreciate it. Thanks to Robert Savoie, the truest friend anyone ever had. Thanks to Gary Sheppard for keeping me sane. Thanks to Phil McCausland, because wow, what a guy. Thanks to David Swider, the best boss ever. Thanks to Tom Franklin, friend and fearless leader. Thanks to Jay Watson for the time and edits and difficult questions, most of which I found a way to answer. Thanks to Douglas Ray, my brilliant forever-friend. Thanks to Gerry Wilson and Stephanie Seabrook, my first guides into the writing world. Thanks to Nic Brown for the wisdom and hangouts. Thanks to Bryony Harrington, who inspired so much in this book. Thanks to Bethan Raines, dear friend so full of grace. Thanks to Alex Taylor for the first read, when it was just an idea. Thanks to Mark Linkous, because his world is one of my favorites to escape into. Thanks to Justin Peter Kinkel-Schuster, whose songs lived in my brain the whole time

I was writing this. Thanks to John Bellairs. Thanks to Lewis Nordan. Thanks to Mermee and Yia Yia, who I miss with all my heart. Thanks be to God. And thanks to all the readers of the world, young and old. This story is yours.

Turn the page for a sneak peek at Jimmy Cajoleas's next spellbinding adventure.

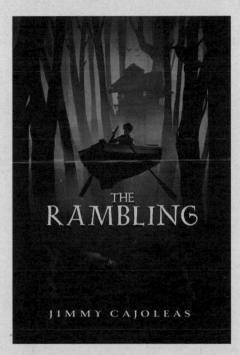

To win at the magical game of Parsnit, you need a good hand and a better story. On his quest to save his father, Buddy Pennington is going to need the hand of a lifetime.

I

IT WAS AFTER MIDNIGHT ON my eleventh birthday when I snuck out of Mom's house and hit the road on the search for my daddy. I packed me a knapsack with some bread and cheese and an apple. I left Mom a note saying, "Sorry, the fire was an accident like I told you it was, I've gone to live with Pop, love you, and may our paths cross again someday soon if the Fates should wish it," which I thought was a pretty nice touch.

I waited till the darkest, blackest time of night, when ugly gray clouds drowned all the moonlight. I snuck right out through my window, didn't wake a soul, dropped down to the earth, and got to moving. I was headed right out of Collardsville, I was, right out of the dirty dull town, taking that muddy moonless road down south.

I hadn't seen Pop in five years, but last I heard he was bunking somewhere down river, near the swamp where I was born and raised, back when he and Mom were still together, back when we were a family. I was going to live with him, same as I always dreamed of doing since we first moved away from him, away from the waters and the swamp, up into town. No more being the town flunky, no more being the shame of my mom. I was on to new things now, to take my place right alongside Pop, who was my hero, one hundred percent, not a doubt in my mind. I was so excited I figured my heart would burst right out of my chest and go running ahead of me.

Pop was something else, I'm telling you. A true wild man, the likes of which were disappearing off the face of this world just as fast as every unmapped forest. Pop was a master of a million arts—a poet, a carpenter, a pugilist of the highest order, and (I had been told) the handsomest man in twelve counties. So what if he was always too busy to come visit me? Why would he, with us living in the town like this, the dirty cluttered cobblestoned roads, boring and respectable, full of fences and gates and doors with locks on them, where a wild soul like Pop couldn't find any freedom or peace?

I loved Mom, quiet and strong as she was, even if she was always harsh on me, even if I couldn't hardly make it through one day without getting punished for something

2

dumb, something bad I didn't even mean to do, it was only my old foul luck getting me in trouble all the time. Mom smelled like eggs and yeast and flour, and every time she hugged you, your clothes got dusted white. But Mom wanted me to become a baker like her. No way in Heaven or Hell was I going to sit in some hot room all day rolling dough. No sir, I knew it in the deep downs of my heart. It was the open road for me, the dusty trail, and best of all the long snaky sneaking river that slithered its way down to the Swamplands, the place Pop most loved, whose waters I'd been born and raised on until I was six and that Pop still wrote me about whenever he was able to write. It was the swamp I missed most of all.

Besides, I couldn't stay in town. Not after what I'd done.

Or at least, what Mom thought I'd done.

It was a long journey I was headed on, let me tell you. Tough too. Wished I could have taken a dirigible like I'd seen float over us once at the county fair. Rides on it cost more than Mom makes in a whole year. Another reason to leave this dopey town.

Nope, instead I walked.

I walked and I walked and I walked.

All night I walked, and come morning I took to hitchhiking. I rode a blind donkey and a bald horse (the owner said he lost his mane in a fight). I rode in a fancy lady's carriage

("Oh you poor thing!" she said) until she got a whiff of how I smelled and made me ride up top with the driver, which was fine with me.

Never had I seen so much of the country, even if it was mostly ugly old farmers wandering through their corn. It took days and days of dreary walking, constant traveling, bumming rides, and sleeping under trees on the side of roads. I kept hoping something wild would happen, something exciting, like maybe I would get robbed or see a ghost or get attacked by wolves. But naw, it was just a long bumpy journey, same as always. I slept under wagons and up in trees and in the tops of barns, always with my eyes open, always looking, looking, looking.

The fields became woods and the ground got murkier, and it was hard, hard to get a ride.

I took up with a fearful old codger on a mule. He slouched and had a beard that grazed his belly. His eyes were bright gold behind his spectacles and he rode all night, barely faster than I could walk.

"What are you so worried about?" I said.

"The Creepy," he said, "lives in the swamp, he does. Eats babies right out of their moms' cribs. Likes to gnaw on dead bones."

"We ain't even in the swamp yet," I said. "We're miles and miles from any notion of a swamp."

"Try telling that to the Creepy."

That night we slept tired and mosquito-bit on the side of the road, and when I woke up my shoes were gone. The old man sat there, chewing on some bread.

"What happened to my shoes?" I said.

"The Creepy," he said, and spat.

Truth was, I was happy to be on the journey, no matter how bad it was. I'd already run away a dozen times, but I always came back because I knew me leaving would break Mom's heart. Besides, she needed help in the bakery. I only ever left for a day or so at a time. So now that I'd gone and wrecked everything, I figured Mom was lucky to be quit of me. I was happy I wouldn't be a nuisance to her anymore. Because let's face it, I was no good as a baker. In fact, I wasn't much good at anything. If you accused me of being a bad kid and a no-good son, well, you wouldn't be too far off the mark.

I will not lie, I was a rambunctious child. I'd ruined pastries, burned tarts, sold moldy rolls to old ladies. I'd stolen a new rabbit coat just to get caught with it. I'd skipped chapel and chipped my tooth on the holy cup. I'd joyridden on neighbors' stallions and climbed to the top of the schoolhouse with an old pirate's spyglass just to see what I could see. I back-talked, spat in public streets. I left the house at all hours and spent my nights with the cows in the pasture up under the big bright moon. Harmless stuff, really, if you want to know the truth about it.

But I had another thing working against me too, and that was my durn horrible luck. For instance, I'd been thrown off no less than six horses, even broke my arm once. I'd contracted whooping cough and pleurisy and hay fever and summer chills and winter fever. I got myself thrown out of school for pushing my teacher down the stairs, but I swear to you it was an accident. I tripped, I did, stumbled right over my own two feet and there was Miss Halloran right in front of me, and I reached out to get a hold of something and down she went. She didn't hardly turn her ankle—it was only three steps down to the grass—but it was enough to get me tossed. Then there was the time Mr. Disley the Potter's wagon tipped and all his oxen got free and his entire stock got smashed and shattered, not a single pot left intact. You don't even want to hear about that one. Rest assured I was innocent entirely. Rest assured not a single person in the village—even my own mom—believed me.

It's embarrassing, all that bad fortune, when your daddy is a famous Parsnit player, renowned for his lucky blood. Why didn't I get that lucky blood, huh? If I had Pop's heart like Mom was always telling me (that's what she said when I did something wrong or got in trouble: "I hoped you'd have my heart at the bottom of it all, Buddy. But nope, you got your daddy's heart. You're your pop's child, through and through"), why didn't I get his lucky blood too? Everything I put my hand to wound up a disaster. So you can understand why perhaps I didn't see much benefit in being good, since it got fouled up every time anyway.

But set the bakery on fire?

That I did not do, I swear to you on a stack of holy books, cross my heart. I did *not*. It just happened.

See, it was early morning and I couldn't sleep.

Mom should have been up already, tending the oven, getting the fires going so they'd be good and hot for the bread. But when I tiptoed into Mom's bedroom, she looked so calm, so peaceful, like she was relaxed for once, not mad or sad or worried about anything. It was like she was smiling almost, and it had been ages since I'd seen her smile. I had seen her up late nights, near to dawn light, cooking up something in the bakery. Whenever I asked her about it, she just said, "Working on a new recipe. Something that will really change stuff for you and me, Buddy." And then she'd put her head down and get back to work. I knew Mom was tired, wore out to the bone. I figured maybe I could get the fires going for her, let her sleep a little bit longer. Everybody knows half an hour's extra shut-eye in the morning is about the best thing there is, especially for a person who works as hard as Mom.

So I went out back to the kitchen, where we kept the two big brick ovens that Mom did all her baking in. It was connected to a storefront where we sold everything.

I pulled up the wood and I lit the kindling and I got the

fire going pretty good. I was poking around with a stick, shoving the coals, making sure the air could get to all the logs, when I happened to glance out the window.

That's when I saw the toad. It was huge, like longer than my forearm, even hunched over, sitting like that. It was the biggest toad I'd ever seen in my whole life. I bet its legs were three foot long each, fully extended.

I know, right? What was a foot-long toad doing in town? What was it doing dry and miles off from any water, croaking away on my windowsill?

It blinked at me.

I realized it only had one big baby-blue eye staring at me, right in the center of its forehead. Must have been hexed. I crossed myself six times and spit like you're supposed to.

That toad stared and stared.

I felt dizzy, strange, like I needed a glass of water, like I'd better sit down.

I'm not sure what happened after that. I guess I blacked out. Because when I came to, the stick I was poking the fire with had caught, and it was leaning against a pile of old empty flour sacks Mom had left lying around.

I don't need to tell you the whole thing was already blazing.

I tried to put it out. I *did*. But before I could make much of a dent in it, Mom came running in, screaming.

"Put it out, Buddy!" she hollered. "Oh Lord God in

Heaven help us, you lit the bakery on fire!"

Mom came back with a bucket of water and a big old blanket. The fire wasn't huge, and the bakery was built pretty sturdy with brick. A couple of the neighbors had run in to help (you know how that word *fire!* can spread faster than the flames themselves). Only half the bakery burned down. It didn't even reach the upstairs, where we lived, where Mom had been sleeping. I counted that a blessing, I did.

'Course I couldn't find the toad that had mesmerized me with his one jeweled eye, and when I tried to tell Mom about it, all she did was mutter to herself, like I wasn't even there.

"I have had all I can stomach," whispered Mom, tears rolling down her cheeks. That was a big deal, and it scared me a little. Never before had I seen my mom cry. She was tough, she was, and quiet. The most you'd ever get out of her was a little chuckle here and there, or a straight-line kind of frown. "I try and I try and I try, and nothing works. I can't even sleep in an hour without it all coming to ruin."

"But Mom," I said. "There was this toad . . ."

Mom shushed me.

"It ain't worth arguing about, Buddy," she said. "Not now. But rest assured, you and me are going to have us a talk tomorrow, and I'm afraid you won't like what you're going to hear."

I'd be a liar if I said that didn't hurt. In fact, it hurt so bad I knew there was no way I could stay at home any longer, not the way I always wrecked things, not how hard I made Mom's life. It hurt me to leave, especially on my birthday, but I also knew I didn't have much of a choice in the matter.

And so what? Life was one big stretch of hurts until your luck turned, until that long golden flip of the coin landed heads up for once. Now, my journey was nearly over. After a whole week of plugging along on that dusty old trail, I was getting close. I had passed through the woods, come into open land. I was in the Riverlands now, where last I heard Pop was living. The hills got hillier and the valleys grew steeper. The road was less crowded, and strange-looking men wandered about, gruff and unshaven. Everything started to smell like fish.

I was headed to Pop's house, and maybe I was the happiest kid in the whole world.